HATTIE BROWN VERSUS THE CLOUD SNATCHERS

CLAIRE HARCUP

AGORA BOOKS

ABOUT THE AUTHOR

Claire Harcup lives in London. Her picture book *This is The Kiss* was published by Walker. *Hattie Brown versus The Cloud Snatchers* is the first of a trilogy.

 twitter.com/Claire_Harcup

ALSO BY CLAIRE HARCUP

This is The Kiss

Hattie Brown versus the Cloud Snatchers

Hattie Brown versus the Elephant Captors

Hattie Brown versus the Red Dust Army

HATTIE BROWN

versus
the Cloud Snatchers

Claire Harcup

First published in Great Britain in 2020 by Agora Books

Agora Books is a division of Peters Fraser + Dunlop Ltd

55 New Oxford Street, London WC1A 1BS

ISBN 978-1-913099-66-4

To Michael

1

The day Hattie Brown got pulled through the fridge was the same day everything started to disappear from the house. And yet another day when she'd had to force her mother to eat.

The clock on the kitchen wall showed it was long past lunchtime, but Hattie's mother hadn't stirred from where she was sitting. In front of her was a piece of paper, half filled with a list. Her fist clawed around a pen, but it didn't move. Just above her head, the clock told Hattie that her mother had been in the same position — without even a twitch — for nearly five minutes.

'Mum,' Hattie said sternly. It was best to be stern when her mother got like this.

The statue that was Stella Brown didn't respond.

'Mum — it's time to eat.'

This time Hattie's mother put the pen down. Slowly. Very slowly. She looked over to Hattie. 'I'm not hungry,' she told her in a voice that had all the happiness squeezed out of it.

'You've got to eat.' Hattie started to tug at the knot in the plastic bag that held the bread. She took the top slice and laid it on a plate. 'Peanut butter, jam or cheese?' she asked, glancing back at her mother as she opened the fridge door.

There was a noise. But her mother's mouth hadn't moved. And anyway, it didn't sound like the kind of noise her mother would have made. It was like a scuffling. And it sounded like it was coming from the direction of the fridge.

'Peanut butter, jam or cheese?' Hattie tried again. She turned back to the fridge. 'Mum, what do you want in your sandwich?'

'I don't care. Whatever you like.'

Hattie felt her jaw tense. This was The Gloom speaking, not her mother. When she wasn't in the grip of The Gloom, Hattie's mother cared what she ate very much. She could make a chocolate digestive disappear in two bites. And she'd been known to walk half a mile out of her way for a cream cake. But The Gloom stole her taste buds as well as her smile.

'I'll give you cheese.' As Hattie reached towards the fridge to get it, something on the middle shelf moved. That was impossible. She frowned and looked again. Everything seemed normal. Perhaps the fridge light had flickered, playing tricks on her.

Her hand stretched further and she picked up the butter dish. It was empty apart from the tiniest smear around the sides. But she'd put a new block on the dish just a little while ago. At least she was pretty certain she had. Her hand hovered as she wondered whether to take the dish away and wash it, and then she heard another sound. Like a sharp intake of breath. Had a mouse got inside? Or maybe the fridge was going wrong. It had been making some strange noises. A broken fridge wasn't what her mother needed when she was in this mood.

Hattie put the butter dish back and her hand moved towards the cream cheese. At least if she used that it wouldn't matter that they didn't have any butter.

She closed the fridge door and made up two sandwiches. As her mother's white teeth sank into the white bread to reach the white cheesy paste, Hattie realised her mistake. Ghost meals like this never cheered anyone up.

But her mother's jaw started rotating anyway. And it took three slow cycles before the white food did its trick and brought her back into the world. She tried to smile, but it was pretty feeble. 'You should have some friends round,' she said, trying a bit too hard to sound happy.

'I don't have any friends.' Hattie came back quickly. It was almost true, only more that she didn't dare to have any friends because they might find out about days like this.

'Everyone has friends.'

'Not me. I don't need them.'

A fresh cloud of sadness passed over Hattie's mother's face, and immediately Hattie felt bad for having snapped at her. 'What's on the paper?' she asked to stop her mother going into herself again.

'I was making a list.'

'Of what?'

'The things that keep disappearing.'

Hattie had noticed that things had been disappearing, too. But she'd decided not to say anything. Stella Brown didn't like mysteries. They made her even more anxious than usual.

'The green hand towel's gone. And my blue top. And your scarf.' Her mother paused. 'And your new shoes for school. And your rucksack. And my gloves. And your socks. All of them missing.'

Hattie's mother peered at her daughter suspiciously.

7

'Have you moved them?' It was half accusation, half question.

'No.'

'Well, I haven't.'

For a moment, Hattie wondered whether she should pretend she'd moved all those things after all, just to stop her mother fretting. But she knew that wouldn't help in the end. Her mother would demand that she put every shoe, scarf, and sock back where it belonged, and she couldn't do that because she didn't know where they were either.

'And the butter,' Hattie's mother went on. 'The butter's disappearing from the fridge. YOU must be eating it all.' Her pen waved in Hattie's direction.

So Hattie's mother had noticed the disappearing butter too. That meant she hadn't been the one who was eating it. And if it wasn't Hattie or her mother, then who could it be? They were the only people in the house.

'Have you been eating all the butter?' Hattie's mother asked.

Hattie shook her head and a froth of hair moved with her.

'Then I'm putting butter on to the list of lost things,' Hattie's mother said.

She walked wearily across the kitchen. 'This is going here until we find them.' She took a magnet and slapped the list on to the fridge. It was the firmest Hattie had seen her be all day. Her fist banged against the door.

'Careful.'

Hattie stared at the fridge. As her mother had hit the door, it had spoken. Hattie looked over to her mother. From the look on her face, it was obvious she'd heard the voice too. But that was impossible. Fridges didn't speak.

'Did you hear that?' Hattie's mother asked.

8

'Maybe,' Hattie said. She didn't want to give too much away. Because it really was impossible — wasn't it?

'There was something.' Hattie's mother hesitated. Tentatively, she opened the fridge door and peered inside. Hattie watched her head turn slowly as she scanned the shelves. 'Nothing there,' she said. 'The noise must have been the motor.' She closed the door. 'I'm feeling tired. I think I'll lie down for a bit,' she told Hattie and left the room.

Hattie watched her go. She crossed her fingers and willed her mother to sleep the mood off. This mustn't be one of those times when her mother became so overtaken by The Gloom that she disappeared further and further into herself, as if there was a gaping hole at her centre that was sucking the rest of her in.

Hattie sighed. She picked up the cream cheese container and opened the fridge door to put it away. But this time she saw the thing that moved. She blinked, not believing what she was seeing, and got as far as saying, 'it's an ele ...'

Then something pulled her into the fridge — and beyond.

2

Beyond the fridge was very beyond. So beyond that Hattie felt her eyeballs pinned back in their sockets. So beyond that her knees felt like they were about to fold the other way. So beyond that her belly button seemed to be unknotting. Don't undo, thought Hattie, because in this weird rush that's pushing and pulling my body all over the place, you may be the only thing that's keeping my insides inside.

She closed her eyes while she somersaulted three more times. As she spun round, she remembered that, just before all this started, she might have seen a tiny elephant sitting on a butter dish. And this topsy-turvy sensation, which sent shocks through her arms and legs and round and round the edges of her ears, might have something to do with that elephant.

'Hold on tight. We're almost through,' she heard a voice say and then something tugged at her arm, almost wrenching it from its socket.

'Brace yourself. Landings are always bumpy,' the voice continued.

The voice probably said more, but the gale of wind in her ears pushed all other sounds away. Then, as if something had disappeared from underneath her, she tumbled to the ground, thudding squarely on her bottom.

'Oh.' She waited to see if that was the end. And when she'd decided that it was, and her necklace, which she could feel spinning around her neck had settled, she said 'oh' again.

'Are you all right?' The voice was back.

'I think so.' Hattie decided she could probably open her eyes now. And when she did, she realised she was sitting in the middle of a big puff of red dust. In front of her, with its trunk wrapped around her other wrist, was an elephant. But it wasn't the one she'd seen in the fridge, it was ...

'Big elephant,' she said, noticing how woozy her voice sounded.

The elephant flicked its trunk to release her. Ears flapping, it stomped over to a tree on the edge of what seemed to be a forest. Fanning out from the tree's centre, like ribbons on a maypole, were tendrils of ivy. The elephant tugged at one of them and started to pull. From where Hattie was slumped, it looked as though the tree had bowed to let the elephant snap it off.

'B ... big elephant.' She pointed to the creature as it plodded back towards her, trailing the ivy behind it. 'But I saw a very small elephant.'

'That was when I was in your realm,' the elephant said, smiling. 'If I was this size there, I wouldn't be able to fit in a fridge.'

'No, I suppose not,' said Hattie, thinking that if her brain didn't feel so befuddled, she might have more to say to an elephant who snatched people through fridges and who talked. Actually talked. But her head *was* befuddled and the big talking elephant, who made her feel sicker every time it moved, was busy. It seemed to be wrapping one end of the ivy around her wrist. Even in her befuddlement that didn't make sense. It had just set her free. But she could feel the ivy tickling her skin, so this wasn't just her imagination. The elephant was holding the other end of the ivy with its trunk. She was like a dog on a lead.

'Why are you doing that?' she asked, trying to stop her words bumping into each other.

'I have to be careful. You might run away,' the elephant said.

With the way Hattie felt, that didn't seem very likely.

'When your eyes have uncrossed, we'll be off,' the elephant said.

'Off to where?'

'The city.'

Hattie couldn't help thinking that the elephant was assuming she knew an awful lot of things. 'And where are we now?'

'Somewhere-Nowhere.'

'Where's Somewhere-Nowhere?' Her hands went clumsily to her pockets. It was okay. The torch, hair grips, magnifying glass, carrier bag and everything else that made her pockets permanently bulge were still there.

'Here. It'll all make much more sense once your brain's stopped spinning. It won't be long now.' The elephant's eyes looked beyond Hattie, sweeping the landscape as though he was searching for something. Hattie followed his gaze, blinking hard as she tried to get used to the glare from the cloudless blue sky. Everything around her looked as though it could do with a good drink — from the brown tips of the grass at the edge of the path, to the leaves of the trees that looked as though they'd crumble if she tried to touch them.

'Why did you bring me here?' Hattie asked, noticing that the trees behind the elephant seemed to be moving differently from any trees she'd seen before. Their trunks swayed and arched as if they had waists. The movement made her feel even sicker.

'Because you can see me,' the elephant replied, turning to look over his shoulder.

'What do you mean I can see you? Of course I can see you.'

'But you saw me in the other realm. Humans can't see us when they're in their own realm. They can hear us, but we're invisible. But you — you could see me. That's why I had to act quickly. Because you could be ...'

The elephant stopped and looked at her intently, staring deeply into her eyes. 'They're not crossed any longer. That means we can get moving — and not soon enough.' The elephant's trunk wrapped around her waist, and she was swept into the air and on to its back. 'I've got the ivy, but you still need to hold on tight,' it called as it set off down a dry rust-coloured path that ran alongside the trees. Her body bounced with every galumphing stride, and she flung her arms around the elephant's neck to stop slipping on the leathery flank of its body. Where was she and what was happening? She opened her mouth to say something but eddies of red dust billowed back in her face, making her choke.

She was about to try again when she heard a high-pitched wail. 'Victor, Victor, you scoundrel. Bring her back this instant, by all the powers invested in me by the Guild of the Knight Dragons.' The trees seemed to stand to attention as the words pierced the air.

'Hold tighter,' the elephant shouted. And he charged into the forest, taking Hattie with him.

3

'Dragon? Did you say dragon?' Hattie shouted at the elephant as he sped deeper into the forest, swerving left and right to avoid the lower branches of the trees.

'Yes — and we don't want him to catch us,' said the elephant.

'But dragons don't exist.' Hattie twisted to see behind them, wondering how on earth she was going to get back to her mother if they were travelling so far away from where she'd arrived.

'Dragons exist all right, though the world would sometimes be a lot easier for us elephants if they didn't.'

A terrible thought crept into Hattie's brain. 'So if the dragon exists, does he breathe fire?'

The elephant gave a tuneless snort, as though he was blowing badly through a tuba. 'They can, but the Code of the Knight Dragons stops them unless it's in defence of our realm.' He ducked under a branch. 'We can't let him catch up,' he shouted.

'But why does he want to catch you?'

For the first time, the elephant slowed. 'It's you he

wants,' he said.

Hattie felt her stomach lurch as she began to feel sick again. A dragon was after her. That sounded scary, even if, by some code she'd never heard of, that dragon wasn't allowed to breathe fire all over her.

'But why does he want to catch me?' she asked.

'Because he doesn't think you should be here.'

Hattie wasn't sure that she should be there either. She was pretty certain she should still be at home with her mother.

'Sir Gideon — that's the dragon — was in your house when I took you, so he thinks he'll be blamed,' the elephant continued.

Hattie tried to take in what she'd just heard. A dragon in her house. In her house in Worcester. A dragon side by side with her and her mother. No, that wasn't possible. Surely she'd have noticed that. 'There can't have been a dragon in the house,' she said.

'Did lots of things go missing?' the elephant asked.

Hattie thought back to the list her mother had slammed on to the fridge door just before all this strangeness had started. 'Yes,' she said. 'Even the butter went.'

The elephant flapped his ears and gave a small cough. 'Actually, that was me,' he said in an apologetic voice. 'But the rest was Sir Gideon. He was looking for something.'

'What was he looking for? And did he find it?'

'A lost seal, and not as far as I know.'

Hattie didn't know what a lost seal was. She didn't even know if it was good or bad that he hadn't found it. 'But if he was in the house, we'd have seen him,' she said.

'Not necessarily,' the elephant said. 'The knight dragons are very small.'

'And is he very big now?' Hattie imagined terrifying

talons swooping down on her shoulders as the dragon attacked her from above.

'It's only the elephants who change size,' the elephant said. 'The knight dragons are always tiny. And they can be irritating enough small. Imagine what they'd be like if they were large.'

Hattie couldn't really imagine it, but she breathed more easily. Maybe it wasn't quite as bad that a dragon wanted to catch her as she'd first thought.

The elephant took a sharp left, powering further into the forest.

'Ouch,' Hattie said as she scraped her arm on a branch. 'Ouch,' she said again as her head yanked back. 'Ouch. Ouch. Ouch. Ouch.'

Only this time she wasn't ouching because of a branch. This time she was ouching because something was pulling at her hair.

'Stop,' she called to the elephant.

But he didn't stop.

'Stop. Please stop.'

The elephant pounded on.

'Mr Elephant!'

The elephant kept on going, but this time he spoke. 'Call me Victor. I think we know each other well enough now.'

The tug on her hair was getting worse. She felt her neck arching backwards. Now she could only look up at the top of the trees.

'Victor! Victor! Something's pulling my hair.'

This time Victor turned. His eyes narrowed and he dug his heels into the ground, sending up a choking red cloud of dust.

'Sir Gideon, let go of the girl this instant!'

4

The dragon didn't let go of Hattie Brown's hair when he heard Victor's command. In fact, it felt to Hattie as though he pulled harder.

He pulled as if his life depended on it. And he pulled until her head crunched right back, and she could see a creature about the size of a sparrow tugging at her hair as if it was a rope. The scales of his powerful body pulsed rapidly between ruby and scarlet as his arched wings whirred frantically. His tail lashed out with every tug. And underneath the crest that rose from the top of his head like a jagged crown, his mouth was pursed into an angry tight knot.

'You can't have her,' Victor shouted, wrapping the ivy that attached him to Hattie tighter around his trunk.

'I can and I will. She was never yours to take from me.' The dragon's wings beat faster as he hovered over Hattie, and his mouth moved as though he was muttering something.

'You're hurting me,' Hattie just managed to say, though her voice mostly came out as a squeak.

The dragon rolled his body so he could twist Hattie's hair tighter.

'Let go of me. That hurts,' Hattie said. 'I'll do whatever you want.'

'Sir Gideon, let her go. In the name of the Guild of the Knight Dragons, stop hurting her,' Victor growled.

But Sir Gideon pulled harder, the colour of his scales settling at scarlet. 'I'll stop hurting her when you let go,' he said. 'You've no right to take her. It was my quest. I swore an oath not to interfere with the human realm unless I found the Lost Seal. I'm going to take her back before anyone finds out she's missing. And before I get thrown out of the Guild of Knight Dragons because everyone thinks I took her, not you.'

'She's not going back.'

'She is.'

'Is anyone going to ask me if I want to go back?' Hattie said in her still-squeaky voice. Tears were prickling her eyes, and she was about to 'ouch' some more when the smell hit her.

It wasn't any ordinary smell.

It was the smell of a sewer that hadn't been cleaned for a thousand years.

It was the smell of one hundred rotten eggs left out in the midday sun.

It was the smell of a monster's armpits.

It was the smell of a million old socks.

It was the smell of an eagle's breath.

It was the smell of a stagnant pond.

It was the smell of a fish's entrails.

It was the smell of rancid cheese.

It was all of these things and more.

Victor obviously smelled it too. His ears were flapping

very fast, as though he was trying to fan something away. The smell was overpowering him.

Hattie felt faint, and she could tell she wasn't the only one. Sir Gideon's grip on her hair weakened. Soon it gave way completely. She watched him flutter down like a leaf in autumn.

He hit the ground just as Victor's bottom landed beside him, and Hattie slid down his side and landed on the ground in a puff of red dust. The leaves on the forest floor crunched as she crushed them.

'Eeuw,' said Sir Gideon.

'Eeuw,' said Victor.

'Eeuw,' said Hattie, clasping her hand to her nose. 'What's that terrible smell?'

'It's the Time Worm. She must be working very close by,' Victor said.

'What does she do that smells that bad?' Hattie asked.

'It's drilling mostly. She drills into your human world.'

Human world? He must be talking about the normal world — Worcester and Britain and the earth and every-where she knew or had read about in books. And if that was the human world, where was this?

'Isn't Somewhere-Nowhere in the human world?' she asked.

'Not in your human world.'

Hattie scrunched up her face in case it made what Victor had just said make more sense. But it didn't. 'Why's she drilling?' she asked. It seemed easier to talk about some-thing practical than to question everything she'd ever thought.

'So she can capture some clouds. Lord Mortimer makes her do it because we don't have enough clouds here. You never get used to the smell, I'm afraid.' Victor shook his trunk as if he was trying to flick the smell out of his nostrils.

'Well, I like the smell, because it stopped you two trying to rip me apart,' Hattie said.

'When are you going to realise that was nothing to do with you?' Sir Gideon said.

'It felt very much to do with me.' Hattie undid the ivy around her wrist and rubbed the back of her neck where Sir Gideon had clung on to her hair. But seeing him look at her, she stopped. She didn't want even a small dragon to think she was weak.

'Humans are so self-centred.' Sir Gideon said, as his eyes darkened, fixing on something over Hattie's shoulder.

Turning, Hattie saw a thick-set man getting off a grey horse just beyond a group of slender trees. He was wearing a burgundy cloak, tied with a bronze brooch. Embroidered in golden thread around the hem of the cloak was a line of woven badges.

'It's one of the Guards of the Realm. They're the army round here,' Victor whispered as Hattie heard Sir Gideon whimper.

'It's the one who sent me on my quest to the human realm,' the dragon moaned.

Good, Hattie thought. At last she'd found someone who'd be able to explain what was going on, and who'd stop this irritating tiny dragon tugging at her hair. She patted her head to see if he'd left any bald patches.

'And this makes things even worse,' Sir Gideon muttered as a small flock of white birds with charcoal-grey beaks and feet swooped down from the trees. Each had a feathery crest on its head, which it flattened as it flew. 'Why do cockatoos always appear when you don't want them? Why can't they keep their noses out of things?'

The guard walked towards them with a squat shuffle. 'Sir Gideon, back so soon,' he observed.

'I finished my quest quickly.'

'And Victor, you're here too,' the guard went on. 'I thought you were gate keeping in the human realm.'

'I'm on holiday.' Victor moved his large bulk to stand between the guard and Hattie.

'I thought you had a holiday not long ago,' the guard replied. With two heavy-footed strides, he stepped round Victor and smirked at Hattie.

'A human-realm child. Hello, child, welcome. May I enquire your name?'

'Don't tell him,' Sir Gideon hissed.

But Hattie wasn't going to be told what to do by this elephant and dragon anymore. Not now she'd met someone who'd be able to take control. 'Thank goodness you're here,' she told the guard. 'I'm Hattie Brown.'

'Hattie Brown.' The guard leaned down and peered first at her and then at Sir Gideon. He reached into the leather satchel that was slung across his chest, pulled out an embossed ledger and started flicking through its pages. 'Hattie Brown,' he said, glancing up at Sir Gideon. 'Let me see.'

As if they were sensing something exciting was about to happen, the cockatoos came closer. The trees seemed to bend towards the guard as if trying to catch his words.

'Hattie Brown. Yes, we sent one of the knight dragons to your house recently.' The guard paused and extended his fat neck. 'We sent ... Sir Gideon.' He turned to him. 'Sir Gideon, I presume you have a permit for Hattie Brown.'

Sir Gideon pursed his mouth and said nothing. His scales took on a deep chestnut blush.

Tapping his finger as he waited for a response, the guard

consulted the ledger again. 'I see she isn't one of the Hundredth Children.' He peered at Sir Gideon as one of the cockatoos perched on his shoulder to look at the ledger for himself.

Why would anyone send a dragon to her house and who were the Hundredth Children? Hattie wondered as the guard looked up at Sir Gideon.

'So have you got a permit?' he asked. He put his finger in the air, as though he had just thought of something. 'Or perhaps she's Nimbus?' His voice was edged with sarcasm.

'Ha ha,' Sir Gideon said. 'Of course Nimbus isn't a girl.'

'So can I see her permit?'

'I ate it by mistake,' Victor said quickly.

'That's very unfortunate,' the guard told him. 'I hope it didn't give you a stomach ache. But Sir Gideon knows that he needs a permit to bring a human into our realm, unless they are one of the Hundredth Children or Nimbus. That makes this situation very unfortunate indeed.'

He took a deep breath so he could bellow the next sentence through the forest.

'Sir Gideon, Victor, and Hattie Brown, you are under arrest.'

5

Under arrest. For a few moments, the guard's words
didn't feel real, even though Hattie knew that's what
he'd said. But then his staff jabbed into Victor's side before
he turned and raised it up, aiming at Hattie's shoulder.

'Move,' he barked. His eyes were dead and cold, and
Hattie felt a shiver electrify her back. She really wasn't sure
how she'd gone from making her mother a cream cheese
sandwich one moment to being arrested in another world
the next. She wished she could close her eyes and whisk
herself back home.

'Move,' the guard said again. He pulled his staff back as
though it was a snooker cue and Hattie's shoulder was the
ball.

'Do as he says,' Victor said softly. He started off, and
Hattie found herself following along the forest path.

'If you hadn't taken her, we wouldn't be in all this trouble.' Sir Gideon was hovering so close to the elephant he
could have landed on his trunk.

The frayed edge of Victor's ear flapped him away. 'And

if you hadn't pulled her hair, I would have been well on the way to the Anywhere Office by now,' he said. 'I would have got her in to the city without any fuss.'

'It was my quest and you spoiled it,' Sir Gideon shouted, his scales pulsing scarlet again. 'You know we only take a Hundredth Child or Nimbus. So why take her?'

'Who are Nimbus and the Hundredth Children?' Hattie asked, determined to get their attention. 'You keep talking about them.'

Victor's gentle eyes looked at her as though it was the most natural thing in the world for her to be beside him. 'They're very important to Somewhere-Nowhere,' he told her.

'And what have they got to do with me?'

'Yes, what? That's the question I'd like answered, too,' Sir Gideon said.

Victor raised his trunk slowly, and Hattie had the strangest feeling that she should know the answer to that already. And yet that was impossible. Of course she couldn't know. Something about this place must be confusing her.

'Why did you take her?' Sir Gideon went on.

'She saw me.'

Of course she'd seen him. It was ridiculous to think she wouldn't. But Sir Gideon didn't seem to think it was so normal. He looked at Hattie with something that might have been awe.

'If she was a boy, I'd say she could be Nimbus,' Victor said.

The scales on Sir Gideon's back became a vivid purple. He continued staring at Hattie in a way that was now making her feel quite uncomfortable. 'But she's a girl,' he said.

A commotion that was happening somewhere in the

forest close by pulled their attention away from Hattie. 'Shhh,' Victor said. 'What's that?'

They all stopped. From somewhere to their left, they could hear the brittle sound of dry twigs being trampled underfoot. Suddenly, a man dressed in the same uniform as the guard strode out of the trees and on to the path. He grunted as he wrestled with something under his arm. It was wrapped in his cloak and a long red tassel hung from whatever it was, brushing the dust around his feet. Both ends of the cloak were flapping so hard that it took Hattie some moments to realise the tassel was a plait of long red hair, and that the thing fighting with the guard was a girl of about eleven. A girl about her own age. For a few seconds, the girl's terrified eyes locked with Hattie's.

'What's he doing to her?' Hattie cried out as Victor stepped quickly to block her view.

She tried to step round him, but he moved again. 'Let me see,' she said. 'I need to see what's going on.' She darted the other way, but he was quicker than he looked. Again he blocked her. And again. And again. She tried to run the other way, but Victor's huge grey belly was like a wall in front of her. She darted back, and this time he didn't try to block her.

'They've gone!' she said. There wasn't even the crunch of leaves under foot to tell her which way they were heading through the trees. 'What was he doing to her?' she demanded.

'I didn't want you to see that,' Victor said.

'But I did see that, so who is she?'

Victor looked very serious, and the feeling that Hattie should know anything about this place vanished entirely. Instead, dread crawled through her.

'She's someone who will help the Realm,' Victor said.

'She didn't look like she wanted to help.'

Victor flicked his tail as sadness clouded his face.

'Who is she and what's he going to do to her?'

As Hattie's voice rose, the guard swished his staff so it thwacked between them. 'Stop,' he bellowed. 'Prisoners should be orderly. Prisoners shouldn't shout. Prisoners should ...'

But Hattie couldn't hear what else he thought prisoners should be or do because a whirring sound filled her ears. Something soft brushed her cheek. Something feathery. A cockatoo was so close that one of his wings stroked her face. Soon he was joined by other cockatoos, and before long she was surrounded by a squadron of them. The pale feathery crests on their heads rose as they inspected her through sharp, dark eyes.

The first cockatoo thrust his face into hers. 'Who you?' he demanded.

What was happening now? And why was this bird looking so stern? The dread clutched her stomach tighter. Was this feeling something to do with the red-headed girl? It had appeared around the same time.

'Who you?' the cockatoo demanded again.

'Hattie Brown.' Hattie decided she'd better smile at him, but his fierce expression didn't soften.

'Where from?' he asked.

'Worcester,' Hattie said.

There was a murmur of approval from the cockatoos. Or possibly it was disapproval. It was difficult to tell. Whichever way, Hattie decided she was going to keep being friendly.

'Why here?' the cockatoo continued in a sing-song voice.

'I don't really know,' Hattie admitted.

The cockatoo bent its head so its beak was at right angles to Hattie's nose. 'Why hair so odd?' With a quick dart of his beak, the cockatoo plucked a strand from her head. Immediately, he spat it out. 'Bad hair,' he said in disgust, his black tongue waggling at her. 'You need crest.'

As he said it, his own crest fell and rose again, to show Hattie its full magnificence. He nodded at the rest of the flock.

Two cockatoos swooped towards her. They started to pluck at her head.

What was it about this place and her hair? She braced her legs in case she found herself in the middle of another tug of war. But the only thing she felt was a sharp snapping around her head as the birds fluttered and flustered around her. As they moved, they muttered, 'Who you? Who you?' in a low chorus.

I've already told you, she almost muttered back to them, before telling herself that she was imagining things.

The birds pulled her hair back from her face, and the skin tightened across her forehead. Suddenly the top of her head felt taller.

'There,' said the cockatoo. He nodded to one of the other birds, who plucked a leaf from a tree. Its brittle underside glistened as he flew towards Hattie. The cockatoo held it up like a mirror and Hattie stared at someone who nearly looked like her. But this nearly Hattie Brown had a strange crest on her head.

'Better,' said the cockatoo. He brushed his wing across the crest so it flexed back. 'Better hair.'

Then he came even closer. 'Better Hattie Brown, whoever you.'

As the cockatoos left her, Hattie realised Sir Gideon was still arguing with Victor.

'You've got to take her back this instant,' Sir Gideon screeched, swooping above Victor's head in frantic circles.

'I'm not going to do that.' Victor's voice was still calm.

'Then I order you by the code of the Guild of the Knight Dragons to give her to me so I can take her back. She's mine.'

'Your codes don't apply to me.'

'I'll do with her what I like.' Sir Gideon's scales flashed scarlet.

'No, I'll do what I like with her,' the guard boomed. He thwacked his staff again at Victor and Sir Gideon. 'This is one thing the knight dragons can't steal the credit for. She belongs to me.'

Hattie didn't think she belonged to anyone. And she was about to tell them that when she saw the cockatoos returning. They were squawking eagerly. They flew up and down above the guard, pirouetting through the air as their calls grew louder and louder.

'What's that? What are they saying?' the guard asked.

Victor turned sharply towards Hattie. His expression was the same as the one she'd seen when he was small and in her fridge. It was a look of disbelief.

'What are they saying?' the guard asked again.

'Trees say Nimbus here. Nimbus in Realm,' the leader of the cockatoos told him. 'Lady Serena found him.' The crests of all the cockatoos stood proud as they nodded to each other.

'But she can't... Lady Serena can't have found him. I'm supposed to find Nimbus,' Sir Gideon wailed, as the trees began a frenzied sway.

'Nimbus. They've found Nimbus.' The guard sank to

his knees and wiped the edge of his cloak across his forehead and over his bulbous nose.

Only Victor didn't seem to be overwhelmed. He stood very still, as if something was puzzling him. He had the look of an elephant who was thinking very fast.

And then, for the second time, he snatched Hattie away.

6

Victor's trunk looped around Hattie's waist, and he threw her on to his back.

'Hold on tight,' he bellowed. 'We're about to go very fast.'

'Where are we going?' Hattie shouted back.

'To Worcester.'

'But you just refused to take me back.'

Victor set off, thundering through the forest, weaving through the trees, away from the guard and the cockatoos. Hattie edged up his back and tucked herself just behind his ears as the red dust billowed around them, bending low so her chin rested on his bristly neck. But every giant elephant footstep flung her up, and she was slipping.

'Victor, slow down,' she called.

'I can't. We've got to get there before she closes up the hole.'

'Get where?' Hattie dug her nails deep into Victor's hide. If someone did that to her she'd stop. But Victor didn't seem to feel a thing. He didn't even flick his crumpled grey ears. And she was still slipping.

'Victor, I'm falling. I'm…'

It was no good. She couldn't cling on any longer. She was going to hit the ground. And it would hurt.

She was bracing herself for the fall when she felt something under her foot. Her leg was being pushed back up. The tips of Sir Gideon's wings flashed into view beneath her boot.

'Pull yourself up,' he shouted. 'Do what Victor says. This time he might be right.' He drove himself against the sole of her boot, and she scrambled back up.

'Thank you,' she gasped as Sir Gideon flew beside her, panting. 'You're very strong for something so small.'

'You can thank me by going away,' Sir Gideon said. 'And you'd better hold on tightly for this bit as well,' he added.

'Why?' Hattie asked, just before the smell hit her.

It was the smell of a sewer that hadn't been cleaned for a hundred years.

It was the smell of one hundred rotten eggs left out in the midday sun.

It was the smell of a million old socks.

And even though it wasn't as bad as the last time she'd smelled something like this, Hattie went 'eeuw' and felt herself go woozy.

Sir Gideon plucked two bristles from Victor's hide and handed them to her. 'Put these in your nostrils. It will help.' Then he frowned. 'I hope the fact the smell isn't that bad doesn't mean she's closed the hole.' He flew close to Victor's face. 'Faster. Faster,' he urged.

'I'm very well aware of the danger,' Victor told him. And he charged on. He charged towards the thing that smelled like an eagle's breath. Towards the thing that smelled like a stagnant pond. Towards the thing that smelled like a fish's entrails. Towards the thing that smelled like rancid cheese. He charged on and on until they came to a gelatinous mound covered in purple-grey blotches. It looked as though someone had dumped a huge pile of dough on to the ground and made it into the shape of an enormous worm. Only, Hattie realised as she stared harder, that was exactly what it was. It was a worm that stretched high up into the sky. From where Hattie was looking, it was impossible to tell where its chest ended and its neck began.

A large bulging net bobbed by the worm's face. It was tethered by a rope to a rock and appeared to be full of cotton wool. As they approached, the worm turned so that Hattie saw a large hole in the sky, flickering with light. Two fleshy lips pulsed in their direction. Above the lips, two sad eyes stared down at Hattie. *Nothing in this place was normal,* Hattie thought. *Nothing at all.*

'The Time Worm,' Victor whispered. Then he said, 'Marcia, we need your help.'

The Time Worm shook her head, spraying saliva from her lips.

Please no, Hattie thought as she ducked to get out of the way.

'I can't help anyone anymore,' the Time Worm said in a mournful voice. 'I've failed.'

'Nonsense,' said Victor. 'Humour her, humour her,' he hissed under his breath at Hattie and Sir Gideon.

'You don't understand what it's like to be me,' the Time Worm said.

'Marcia, you can help an old friend.' Victor smiled.

'No one should want to be my friend. Lord Mortimer has punished me, and I deserve to be punished,' the Time Worm said.

'Who's Lord Mortimer?' Hattie whispered to Sir Gideon.

'He's the ruler of Somewhere-Nowhere. And he's not a very understanding man.'

'I'm not worthy of being a friend,' the Time Worm wailed. Another globule of saliva escaped from her mouth to the ground and immediately a purple flower sprang up where it had fallen. 'Go away,' she said. 'Don't let anyone see you talking to me or they'll punish you. I have to go back to work.'

She turned and clamped her lips down on the hole's edge. Instantly, the gap in the sky became smaller.

'No!' Victor and Sir Gideon yelled together.

'We need to get this girl back to the human realm,' Victor explained.

So that was why they brought me to the Time Worm, Hattie thought. That made sense for Sir Gideon. He'd never wanted her in Somewhere-Nowhere. But why had Victor changed his mind? If he hadn't wanted her there, why had he pulled her through the fridge in the first place?

'The Hundredth Children don't go back. They go to Lord Mortimer,' the Time Worm said. She looked as though just this fact might make her cry. 'That's what Lord Mortimer wants. And Lord Mortimer always gets what he wants.'

'She's not one of the Hundredth Children. She's here by mistake,' Victor said.

'Your mistake,' Sir Gideon muttered.

'Human-realm children don't get here by mistake,' the Time Worm said.

'Exactly.' Sir Gideon scowled at Victor.

'I don't think it was a mistake at the time,' Hattie said, thinking it was about time she got to tell this blubbery creature her version of what had happened. 'You see, I opened the fridge and ...'

'Be quiet,' Sir Gideon said.

'I was just trying to explain.'

'A human-realm child who shouldn't be here. Lord Mortimer won't like that,' the Time Worm said, shaking her head so drops of saliva showered Hattie, Victor, and Sir Gideon.

'Exactly,' Sir Gideon said, flicking the saliva off his wings. A small blue flower sprang up in the spot where it hit the ground. 'So we just want to put her back in the human realm and say no more about it. Lord Mortimer need never know.'

'Lord Mortimer would punish me if I helped you.' The Time Worm's attention went back to the hole, and her body arched. 'I see a cloud,' she said as she peered through. 'I'll just take one more before I close up.' Her lips elongated, as though she was going to kiss something on the other side, and she leaned closer to it.

'We've got to get her to do it,' Victor whispered to Sir Gideon.

'She's scared,' Sir Gideon said. 'But we're the ones who should be scared. Once she's got the cloud through, she'll close up the hole and then we'll have no way of sorting this out.' He paused, thinking. 'Maybe we could fling the girl through before Marcia knows what's happening.'

'Fling me through. What, like a ball?' Hattie said. How could they talk as if it didn't matter what happened to her as long as they got rid of her?

'A bit like that,' said Sir Gideon.

'And where would I land? Back in my house?'

Sir Gideon scrunched up his face. 'I don't think so. It

depends where the Time Worm is drilling. You'll just be somewhere that's not here, and that's all we can hope for.'

'What about what I can hope for?'

Victor positioned himself at an angle to where the Time Worm was working. 'It's not going to be easy. I don't want to hurt her. Maybe if I just fling her as far as I can. Then you can fly into her back and push her through the last bit.'

Sir Gideon nodded.

'Don't I get any say?' Hattie asked.

'No,' Sir Gideon said.

'I'm sorry.' Victor's forehead wrinkled. 'But this is better than what might happen if you stay.'

The Time Worm was beginning to inch backwards. Her lips were retracting through the hole. Hattie could see the fluffy edge of a cloud emerging like a plume of candy floss.

The Time Worm pulled back, and more came. Then more and more, until a small cloud popped through the hole and bounced up into the air above them.

'I'll put it in the net and log it after I've closed the hole,' the Time Worm said. 'Logging clouds always takes longer than anyone thinks.'

'Get ready,' Victor told Sir Gideon. His trunk came over his back searching for Hattie.

This had to be a joke. No one threw children through holes into other worlds. 'Are you really sure I'll be okay?' Hattie asked.

'We think you probably will be,' Sir Gideon said.

'I'll be as careful as possible.' Victor wrapped his trunk around Hattie's waist as the cloud hovered above them. His trunk tightened around Hattie's body.

So this wasn't a joke. He really was going to do it.

'Ready?' Sir Gideon checked.

'Ready,' Victor said.

'Not ready,' Hattie shouted.

A shadow passed over her as the cloud settled above them. A raindrop splashed her face. *Even the cloud's sad for me*, she thought and squeezed every muscle in her body tight, waiting for what was about to happen.

Another drop fell on Victor's head. He flinched. Another three raindrops fell and he looked up. As more drops started to trickle down his trunk, his ears began to flap.

'Now,' Sir Gideon urged.

But Victor didn't move.

'Now!' Sir Gideon yelled. He tugged at Hattie's arm, as if he was going to throw her himself. *Here we go*, Hattie thought. *They're about to send me goodness knows where. And goodness knows why*. She closed her eyes.

But instead of hurtling through the skies into the gap and beyond, she heard Victor yelling at the Time Worm.

'Close the hole! Close it now!'

7

'No, no, no!' Sir Gideon shouted. His scales went from pink to green to blue to brown to crimson to really crimson, to oh-so-very-very crimson. 'No!'

But the Time Worm's mouth was moving across the edge of the hole, sealing it as though she was crimping two pastry edges together on a pie.

'All closed up,' she said dolefully, turning to look at them. She burped. 'Sorry about that. It happens.'

Sir Gideon let out an undignified whimper, and he fluttered to the ground. 'The end. It's the end,' he muttered.

'What happened?' Hattie asked. Her body was tense. She was still half expecting Victor to toss her up in the air, past the purple-grey blubber of the Time Worm and through a hole that might open up again at any moment. And if that happened, she'd be on her way to who knew where.

'You're still here,' Sir Gideon screamed as he fluttered round her face. 'You're not supposed to be here. You're supposed to be anywhere but here. Anywhere but Some-where-Nowhere.'

Sir Gideon turned to face Victor. 'And you stopped that from happening.' Sir Gideon's scales started to change colour again. 'You didn't throw her,' he yelled.

'No, I didn't,' Victor said.

'We agreed.'

Victor looked up at the cloud that was now a little way away from them. 'And then I unagreed,' he said.

'You can't just unagree.'

'Yes I can. I'll show you why.' Victor moved towards the cloud. He waved his trunk. 'Watch,' he told Sir Gideon, positioning himself underneath the cloud.

'Watch what?' Hattie asked. If there was something interesting to see, she wanted to make sure she didn't miss it. She followed Victor's gaze and looked up at the cloud.

And as she watched, the cloud shivered, and a small shower of rain fell on them. Where the drops hit the ground, delicate yellow flowers sprang up from the soil, like flashes of gold in the red dust.

Sir Gideon gasped, and the Time Worm made a sound like a reverse burp.

'It rained on her,' Sir Gideon said.

'That's why I didn't catapult her back into the human realm,' Victor said.

'But it wasn't much.' Sir Gideon's colour had settled at green.

'More than I've ever seen in one go like that.'

Sir Gideon and the Time Worm were staring at Hattie, and she wasn't sure she liked it. They were staring at her in a way that made her skin tingle.

'Can someone tell me what's happening?' she said. 'First you wanted me to be here, then you didn't. Then you wanted to throw me out of your world like I was a ball, then you didn't. What's going on?'

'It rained, that's what's going on. It rained from the cloud,' Sir Gideon said.

'That's what clouds do,' Hattie said. 'They take up water and then they use it to make rain.'

'Not here,' Victor said. 'Here the clouds don't rain.'

'Not unless ...' the Time Worm started.

'Shhh,' Victor said.

'But the cloud rained on you.' The Time Worm stared even harder at Hattie. She turned her face up to the cloud, which was floating away from them. 'If we had another one, we could see if it was a one-off.'

'We can wait for the next one.' Hattie followed her gaze, thinking it was probably a good thing that she wasn't on a solo flight to a mystery place, but she still needed to get home.

'There aren't many clouds here,' Victor said. 'In fact, there are only the ones the Time Worm sets free.'

'I'm meant to send nets with the clouds in them to the Cloud Keeper near the city.' The Time Worm's large bulging eyes blinked slowly as she spoke. 'But every now and then I let a cloud go. I always say it's an accident, but it's so everyone outside the city can have a bit of rain too. I shouldn't. If Lord Mortimer catches me, I'll be punished.'

'He won't catch you. No one who lives outside the city would tell. They're too grateful.' Victor smiled.

'What's the point of releasing the clouds if they don't rain?' Hattie asked.

'We throw stones and sometimes that gets a few drops out of them.' Victor's expression darkened. 'To get water for the city they have other methods. But you made it rain without us having to throw stones. No one's ever done more than a few drops at a time.'

'But it wasn't much. The shower didn't last long.'

'That shower counts as a miracle around here.'

'It could have been the change in the temperature,' Hattie said. 'The cloud's just been pulled through from — well — I don't know where. But wherever it was, the temperature could have been different enough for rain to start when it got here.'

The Time Worm nodded. 'The human-realm child may be right, Victor.'

'Hattie,' said Hattie. 'I'm called Hattie.' When would they start treating her like she was more than a curiosity?

'What an unfortunate name,' the Time Worm said. 'I hope it doesn't make you sad.' She turned to the others. 'I'd like it to be the human Hattie. But it can't be. It must be a coincidence. The cloud was adjusting to the new world, like the human Hattie said.' The Time Worm's eyes brimmed with tears. 'So now she's trapped for nothing.'

'Did you say I'm trapped?'

'Yes, you can't go back until a new order for clouds comes through from Lord Mortimer, and who knows when he'll ask me to drill again. He doesn't like me to do it too often, in case the people in the human realm notice.' Her voice became higher and higher. 'I'm sorry, human-realm child. I'm sorry, human Hattie. They shouldn't have condemned you like this. And all for nothing.' Tears swelled in her eyes. 'And now I feel so sad. I don't think I can go on.' The tears started to spill over the rims of her eyes. 'I could have saved you. I could have saved you,' she wailed. 'They've been so cruel.' She began to rock back and forth.

'Marcia, the cloud isn't a coincidence,' Victor said. 'When I was in the human realm, she saw me.'

The Time Worm's wails stopped. Her body swayed unsteadily. 'It's a miracle,' she managed to say before she fell flat on her stomach.

8

'It's not a miracle. It's a disaster.' Sir Gideon had turned crimson again. He stood on Victor's back and stamped his foot.

Unconcerned, Victor picked up a branch from the dusty ground and started to fan the Time Worm's face.

'Marcia, are you all right? That was quite a fall.'

The Time Worm raised her head. 'The bruises will be no more than I deserve for letting the cloud go. Lord Mortimer will think I'm doing it on purpose.'

'But you are,' Sir Gideon said.

'You're right.' The Time Worm's head flopped on to the ground again, sending blubbery shock waves down the length of her body.

'A little while ago someone mentioned that I'm trapped. Would anyone like to talk to me about what that means?' Hattie asked.

'Yes, you're trapped,' the Time Worm wailed, tears swelling again in her sorrowful eyes.

'But I've got to get back,' Hattie said. 'For my Mum.' Her voice trailed off as she thought about her mother. How long had she been in this strange world? It must have been three or four hours at least. Her mother would be frantic. She wouldn't know what to do when she found Hattie wasn't at home. What would she imagine had happened to her? There would be nothing. Not even a note. Just no Hattie anywhere. 'I can't stay here,' Hattie said.

'You're trapped for who knows how long,' the Time Worm said.

'That's if —' Sir Gideon started.

'Quiet,' Victor said.

'That's if what?' Hattie asked.

'That's if they don't get you first,' the Time Worm wailed. 'I promise to come to your memorial service. I'll cry for you every day.'

'But a moment ago you said I was a miracle. And now you're talking as if I'm going to die,' Hattie said.

'Oh, but you are a miracle. And that's what's so sad. It's so upsetting to think of a miracle human-realm child being dead.'

'Nobody's going to die,' Victor said.

Sir Gideon flew up and hovered by his right ear. 'What are you proposing we do now you've messed things up for a second time?' he demanded. 'I shouldn't be here with you. I should be with Nimbus. He can't be left with Lady Serena. But I can't be where I belong because I've got to work out what to do with Hattie Brown.'

'Are we all agreed that she's a miracle of sorts?' Victor asked.

'Yes,' the Time Worm said.

'No,' Sir Gideon said.

Victor's ear flapped at Sir Gideon, as if he were a fly that was irritating him. 'Can we at least agree that she's different?'

'I suppose so,' Sir Gideon conceded. 'But she's different in a way that's trouble.' He paused. 'Maybe we can just smuggle her in as one of the Hundredth Children.'

'No, not her.' Victor's voice was sharp.

'Who are the Hundredth Children, and why do you want me to be one of them?' Hattie asked.

Victor looked over to Sir Gideon, as if he was warning him not to say anything, but the Time Worm started talking anyway. 'It's so sad,' she wailed. 'They're human-realm children, just like you. Only they have to be kept in a cage.'

Hattie's throat felt dry. 'That girl I saw — was she one of them?'

'I expect so,' the Time Worm said as Victor moved towards her and swung his trunk across her lips. 'I've said too much,' she sobbed as she realised what he was doing. 'I always say the wrong thing.'

Hattie watched as Victor and Sir Gideon went to the Time Worm. They were comforting her, but no one was trying to comfort Hattie. She was the one who'd been whisked away to a strange world where she'd been argued over and ignored and nearly flung away like a ball before being told that children like her were imprisoned somewhere in a cage. She was the one who had been told she might die. Didn't they realise how that made her feel? She wished Victor would wrap his trunk gently around her to make her feel better. Even a smile from Sir Gideon would help a bit. But she was on her own here, just like she was at home when she was trying to deal with her mother and The Gloom. She'd come to a completely different world but nothing had really changed. She still had to deal with things alone.

Behind her there was a rustling of leaves, and she turned to see a group of trees bending in her direction.

Their branches were curling as though they were beckoning, the silver under-sides of the leaves making them twinkle with sparkling light. She might as well go to them. There was nothing that made her want to stay with a dragon and an elephant who couldn't agree, and an over-sized worm who wouldn't stop crying. They weren't about to help her get home. She might as well take her chances somewhere else.

While Victor and Sir Gideon were distracted by the Time Worm, Hattie Brown tiptoed away and went towards the beckoning branches.

9

The closer Hattie got, the more agitated the trees became. Their branches swayed and danced, enticing her to keep going. And the further she went into the forest, the fainter Sir Gideon and Victor's voices grew. When she came to a clearing, she couldn't even hear the Time Worm's wails any more.

She'd got away from the cross dragon who wanted to put her in a cage. But now that she was truly on her own in a strange world where nothing seemed to be what she expected, it was hard to know what she was supposed to do next.

Before she had time to decide, a branch tapped her on the arm. Hattie jumped back and it tapped her again. It moved upwards and, as it rose, the branches of the other trees rose too. Soon they all pointed to the sky and sunshine flooded the ground.

Hattie's gaze followed the direction of the pointing branches, up to a blue sky that seemed to go on forever. Eventually the trees began to sway. The one whose branch had tapped her on the arm bowed towards her.

'What are you trying to tell me?' Hattie asked.

The branch danced around her face, and Hattie noticed how much drier it looked than the branches of the trees she passed on her way to school. The branch flung itself towards the sky again. Only this time the perfect blue was interrupted by a single wispy cloud. As the cloud got closer to where Hattie was standing, the trees began to rustle. Soon it was as though an anxious wind rushed through their dry leaves.

Then, just as the cloud was exactly over Hattie's head, the rustling stopped.

Every branch on every tree was completely still. Waiting.

The cloud shuddered. It shuddered again. Then a flurry of raindrops fell at Hattie's feet. Where they hit the ground, flowers sprang up. And as their stems twisted towards Hattie's legs, she could hardly tell the real flowers from the ones that patterned the boots her teachers were always telling her she shouldn't wear to school.

The leaves in the treetops made a noise that sounded like whispering, and Hattie stared up at the cloud, trying to understand what was supposed to happen next.

The leaves of the trees rustled expectantly around her.

An idea came to her. It was something she'd never dream of doing when she was at home, but it felt right here — like it was something she was meant to do. She raised her arms to the cloud and the forest seemed to take a deep breath.

As her hands went high, the cloud shuddered again. Then a splattering of drops fell on to her forehead and dribbled down her nose.

The tree that had touched her arm bowed in her direction.

This was strange. Here things seemed to obey her. At home she could stare out of the window for hours, wishing it would stop raining, and nothing happened. But here she could make rain and was called a miracle.

She threw her arms up like actors did in films. 'I order you to rain,' she said in her deepest, most important voice. And then she waited.

But nothing happened. This time the cloud didn't even shiver and, after a few moments, it floated away.

As it left, the rustling started again. It felt as though every tree was staring at her disapprovingly. If leaves could tut, that was what they'd be doing, Hattie thought as she looked round, wondering what she should do now. At the edge of the clearing, she noticed a bench that she hadn't seen before. She walked over and sat down heavily, kicking her feet against the wooden legs while she decided what happened next.

'Ouch,' a voice said.

'Who said that?' Hattie asked.

'I did,' the voice replied.

Hattie looked around her. She couldn't see anyone or anything that could have spoken to her.

'Are you a tree?'

'Certainly not. Well — not anymore.'

'But I can only see trees.'

'That's nice, isn't it? You think about the trees and just ignore me. I call that rude.'

'Let me see you.' Hattie stood up on the bench to get a better view.

'There you go again, and without a "please, may I". So rude.'

'But I'm not trying to be rude,' Hattie said.

'And you're not trying to be polite either. Careful where you put those muddy shoes.'

'Where are you?' Hattie asked.

'You're standing on me. And by the way, you seem to have some elephant bristles stuck up your nose.'

Hattie looked down as she tugged the bristles from her nostrils.

'But benches don't talk.' She sat down again.

'Oh yes, go on insulting me, why don't you? First you don't ask before slamming yourself down on my back. Then you kick me. Then you trample red dust all over me. And now you doubt that I can talk. You're not exactly making me like you.'

With that a splinter came from nowhere into Hattie's leg.

'Ouch.'

'Pain for a very rude girl.'

'I didn't mean to be rude. But benches don't talk where I come from.'

'I bet they do, only you're too rude to listen. Or maybe you can't hear for thinking about yourself. And it looks like that's not the only thing you can't do.'

'What do you mean?'

'The rain thing. It wasn't very good, was it?'

'There were some drops.'

'We expected more. The cockatoos told us Victor had brought you here without a permit. Why would he do that unless there was something amazing about you? The trees thought you might be able to make it rain. They're very thirsty, you know. But that was disappointing.' The bench gave out a low sigh. 'Very disappointing.'

'Oh.' How stupid she was. Of course she couldn't command the weather. No one could.

Around her, the rustling seemed to be getting louder. The trees had begun to bend. They were leaning in, as if they wanted to hear their conversation.

'I'm sorry to have disappointed you,' Hattie said.

'Most humans are disappointing, in my view. It comes with your species, so I won't go on about it. The trees, however, are a different matter.'

'What do you mean?'

'They don't take kindly to disappointment. And they were looking forward to a good drink.'

'I'm sorry,' Hattie said to the clearing.

'I wouldn't waste your breath,' the bench said.

'Why not?'

'It won't stop them doing it.'

'Doing what?'

'Robbing you,' the bench said.

And with that, Hattie felt the first branch dive into one of her pockets.

10

The tree thieves were quick. Supple branches were in and out of Hattie's pockets in a moment. They frisked her body. They checked her hair. They fumbled behind her ears. And they found all the things her mother always complained shouldn't be in her pockets, as well as the things even she didn't know she had. They found sweet wrappers. And hair grips. And a handkerchief. They found a torch. And a magnifying glass. And a stethoscope. They found a dog whistle. And a carrier bag. And a beaker. But they didn't find what they wanted.

'You've disappointed again,' the bench said as Hattie gazed at the contents of her pocket scattered at her feet.

'Don't they put anything back?' Hattie asked as the branches pulled away.

'Not unless there are exceptional circumstances.'

'And these circumstances aren't exceptional?'

'It seems not.'

'What were you looking for?' Hattie shouted at the clearing.

'Shhhhhh,' the bench said. 'You don't want them to find you.'

'Who?'

'Them. It's my understanding that you're travelling without a permit. You need to be very careful. And anyway, you won't get an answer from a tree.'

'But what were they looking for?' Hattie asked. She was whispering now.

'The Lost Seal.'

'What's that?'

'Oh, you know, only the key to everything.'

'No, really?'

'Really.' The bench snorted. 'They say that if it's back in Somewhere-Nowhere, the clouds will return.'

'How did it get lost?'

The bench sighed. 'I suppose there's no harm in telling you. Part of the seal disappeared after the Battle of the Three Volcanoes, when Lord Mortimer fought his brother, Lord Jasper — only most people round here call him The Traitor, because he was our ruler until he went and married one of you lot.'

'What do you mean "one of you lot"?'

'People from your realm. He went and married one of them, and that didn't go down well with the inhabitants of Somewhere-Nowhere.'

'Don't you like us?'

'It's not so much about liking. More about fear. Everyone's afraid of the humans from your realm. And they thought that if one of them married our ruler, the other humans from your realm would be bound to get to know about us.'

'But I've seen humans here. The guards are human, aren't they?'

'Yes, and so's Lord Mortimer. So's The Traitor himself. But they're all from Somewhere-Nowhere, not from your realm.'

'What's so wrong with us?'

'You'd destroy us.'

'No we wouldn't.'

'Yes, you would. That's what you do — even when you don't mean to.'

Hattie thought for a moment. She didn't like the idea that the inhabitants of Somewhere-Nowhere might be frightened of all the people she knew. And the more she thought about it, the more it didn't make sense. 'So if you don't want us to know about you, why does the Time Worm steal the clouds? And why were Victor and Sir Gideon in my house?'

'We need your clouds.' The bench took another deep breath. 'Plus, Lord Mortimer thinks the Lost Seal might be somewhere in the human world. And until he has the Lost Seal, he can't have complete control over Somewhere-Nowhere. Not everyone thinks he should be our ruler. Some want to lead a rebellion against him, just like he rebelled against his own brother. But if Lord Mortimer has the Lost Seal and the clouds return, he'll be safe. His enemies won't be able to blame him for the drought and raise an army against him.'

Beneath Hattie, the bench shifted, and she felt herself slipping. She stood up.

'Thank you for finally having the manners to get off me,' the bench said.

'But I thought benches were for sitting on.'

'Only if you ask and they say "yes".'

'Sorry,' Hattie said. She put the hair grip and the handkerchief and the magnifying glass into her pocket. And she was just picking up the torch when a voice asked, 'Does it work?'

'Yes,' Hattie said, thinking that the voice didn't sound like the bench.

'Good.' Something snatched the torch from Hattie's hand and turned it on. A bright light shone straight into her eyes, blinding her.

'Who are you?' the voice asked.

'Hattie.'

'Hattie who?'

'Hattie Brown.'

'A human-realm child. Are you one of the Hundredth Children?' The torch shifted slightly, and now that it wasn't shining straight in her eyes, Hattie thought she could see something fluttering in front of her. She blinked some more, to let her eyes adjust, then she saw exactly what it was. Another tiny dragon. Only this one was a beautiful golden colour. And every time she moved, her scales shimmered as though they were sprinkled with gold dust.

Hattie stiffened. Was this dragon going to be like Sir Gideon? Was she going to want to lock Hattie up in a cage? Hattie tried to think what her mother would say in a situation like this. Or what her mother would say when The Gloom hadn't got her. Her feisty mother who didn't mind leaving the house. The mother who was happy to go to the shops. But Hattie's feisty mother was rarer and rarer now, and Hattie's memories of her were hazy. She couldn't easily summon her up as her guide. She'd have to rely on her own instincts instead.

'No, I'm not one of the Hundredth Children.' Hattie tried to sound defiant.

The torch focused back on her face. 'Not one of the Hundredth Children?' The dragon's golden head cocked to the side. 'That's interesting. Do you have a permit?'

'No. Victor brought me here. And a dragon called Sir Gideon.'

'Sir Gideon.' The dragon's voice cackled as the torch began to wobble. 'Sir Gideon!' The torch moved frantically. 'Sir Gideon!' The voice cackled again. 'He brought you here?'

'Not exactly.'

'Then how do you know him?'

'He was in my house.'

'I knew it. I knew it,' the delighted dragon screeched. 'He thought you were Nimbus.'

'Not really.'

'He thought YOU were Nimbus.' The dragon's screech grew louder. 'You with that strange mound of hair on your head and your big bulging pockets.' The dragon swooped down. 'And those clumpy boots. I bet you think they look great because they're covered with flowers.'

Hattie looked down at her boots. 'But I like...' she began.

The dragon darted up again. 'Sir Gideon brought you here without a permit because he thought you were Nimbus,' she said. 'Only you're not.'

'Who's Nimbus, and why's everyone so bothered about whether Sir Gideon thought that's who I am?'

'Nimbus is the heir to the ruler of Somewhere-Nowhere,' the golden dragon told her. 'And I know you're not Nimbus, because there he is.'

Behind her, Hattie heard the bench gasp. The branches of the trees swayed forward to see where the dragon was pointing.

Standing in the dappled light of the forest, watching what was happening, was a boy.

'Hattie Brown,' the dragon said. 'Meet Arthur Handley-Bennett. Meet Nimbus.'

11

A rthur Handley-Bennett put out his hand to Hattie
Brown. It was a confident hand, with the kind of
handshake someone who was the heir to a ruler would have.
It was a firm, bone-crushing, knuckle-crunching handshake.

'Hello,' Hattie said.

'Hello,' Arthur Handley-Bennett said.

Arthur Handley-Bennett didn't look like the kind of boy
who would have a knuckle-crunching handshake. In fact,
Hattie was surprised that any boy would choose to shake
hands with someone they'd just met without being forced
to. It made her look at him with even more curiosity. He was
tall, but he had the thinness of someone much younger than
the twelve or thirteen years she guessed he must be. His
curly dark hair framed wide-set eyes and an even wider
mouth, and as soon as he had said 'hello', his shoulders
dropped into the slight hunch Hattie suspected was most
natural for him. He looked like someone who would be
picked last for the sports team at school, but who wouldn't
mind.

'I've heard about you,' Hattie said. 'We met some cockatoos in the forest who told us you were here. Everyone seems very excited about you.'

Surprise flashed through Arthur Handley-Bennett's eyes, but the golden dragon next to him looked pleased. 'Oh good,' she said. 'So they know. And if the cockatoos know, then everyone will know by now. And did they say who found him? Did they say it was Lady Serena? Did they say it was me?' She took a small bow.

'Yes, they did,' Hattie said.

Lady Serena's scales shone even brighter. 'And does Sir Gideon know I found Nimbus?'

'Yes.'

Lady Serena flew around Hattie and Arthur Handley-Bennett. 'What did he say?' Her wings beat very fast.

Hattie didn't think she much liked the way Lady Serena was acting. And she wasn't going to give her the pleasure of knowing how badly Sir Gideon had taken the news. 'He didn't seem to care,' she said.

'Not care? Of course he cares. He cares very, very much.' Lady Serena flapped around Hattie's head, the diamond-shaped pupils of her eyes growing dense. 'He was pretending not to care, just for your sake.' A cheerful grin passed over her face. 'Inside he was dying. He always is when I get the better of him. And isn't this just the best thing ever? He always said he'd get Nimbus. He got all boasty about it. But Nimbus is with me.'

She circled them both again. 'Come on, you two, no time to lose,' she said. 'We've got to get to the Anywhere Office.'

Hattie wondered whether to refuse. But then she didn't know what she'd do if she did. It would be harder to find a way back to her mother on her own. And if she went with Arthur, at least she'd be with someone who knew how odd things were for her. She wouldn't be completely on her own anymore. She surprised herself as she thought how relieved she felt knowing he was here too. Something about her was lighter. It was strange to feel like that about someone she'd just met.

'How did you get here?' Hattie asked Arthur as they followed Lady Serena.

'It was *weird*,' he said, hunching his narrow shoulders as he emphasised the word. 'I opened the fridge to get some milk, and suddenly I was being sucked right through and there were strange lights everywhere and it felt like I was on a loop the loop. Then I landed in a big patch of red dust next to an elephant and a little tiny dragon.'

Hattie nodded. 'Me too,' she said.

'So where are the dragon and elephant who brought you here?'

'I ran away from them.'

Arthur's eyes widened. 'Did they hurt you?'

'Not exactly. But the dragon wanted to get rid of me and the elephant didn't seem to be able to make his mind up whether he wanted me to stay or not.' She looked around them. 'What happened to your elephant?'

'He left us soon after I got here. Lady Serena said the elephants and the dragons are the only inhabitants of this place who can come to the human realm without dying. Even the humans can't unless they were born there.' Arthur leaned closer to her and lowered his voice. 'Have you noticed how everything's a bit like home yet really not at all? I'm not sure I like it. But Lady Serena says we have to go to the Anywhere Office, so I'm going along with it.' He shrugged. 'I don't really know what else to do.'

They'd come to a dusty red path at the side of the forest. 'What happens at the Anywhere Office?' Hattie asked.

'Lady Serena says it's the main gate to the city,' Arthur said. 'And the only way in if you haven't got a permit to travel inside. But because I'm Nimbus, she says there won't be any trouble getting one.'

'And do you think you're Nimbus?' Hattie asked.

'I think I'm Arthur from Manchester. But I've been practising my handshake, just in case. Did you like it?'

A cockatoo swooped towards them.

'Hello,' Hattie said, recognising one of the birds who'd done her hair earlier. But the cockatoo ignored her. It perched on Arthur Handley-Bennett's shoulder and checked behind his ears.

Arthur winced. 'They keep doing that,' he said. 'Lady Serena says it's because everyone thinks I'm so important here and they're very excited.' He raised his eyebrows. 'Wait until you meet the cockatoos properly.'

'I already have. They did this.' Hattie pointed to the quiff on her head.

'Oh,' said Arthur. 'I wasn't going to mention that. I thought something bad had happened when they pulled you through.' He paused. 'Where did you come from?'

'Worcester.'

'I don't know where that is.'

'Not long now,' Lady Serena called to them. 'The Anywhere Office is just over the brow of that hill where Turnaround Track and Creepalong Lane meet.'

Hattie followed the direction she was pointing, where the dusty red path climbed steeply. At the top of the hill, she saw an elephant. 'Look, there's Victor,' she said.

'That's not Victor. It's one of the other elephants. They look so similar. Victor is the most important of the gate keepers and the wisest, but he's not the only one.' Lady Serena paused. 'Victor is getting weaker, though. He takes everything that happens around here to heart. I suppose one day the stress will kill him,' she said cheerfully. 'If you don't first.'

'What do you mean, if I don't first?'

'I know I like to blame Sir Gideon, but I understand Victor was the one who took you.' She hovered around Hattie's head, a mischievous look on her face. 'That's right, isn't it? So they'll probably punish them both.' She nodded. 'That would be the fairest thing to do.'

Hattie frowned. So Sir Gideon was right to be angry at Victor for bringing her there. No wonder he was so eager to get rid of her.

They'd reached the brow of the hill, and not far below them Hattie saw a crowd standing under a solitary cloud. She hesitated, staring at the ragged group of humans and rabbits who'd gathered together beside some hunched scaly animals with long snouts and thick tails. Pangolins. She'd seen them once on a nature programme, but who'd have thought she'd ever see them for real? The fur on the rabbits was dull and matted, and sprinkled with the same fine coating of dust that seemed to cover everything in Somewhere-Nowhere. And the people were much thinner than the paunchy guard of the realm Hattie had met earlier. They stared up at the cloud with gaunt, tired faces.

'Is that one of the clouds the Time Worm's let go?' Hattie asked.

'You're learning fast.' Lady Serena almost looked like she approved.

A man, dressed in a dirty grey shirt and trousers that must have been two sizes too big for him, launched a stone at the cloud. The woman next to him threw another. Both stones skimmed the bottom of the cloud and fell to the ground.

'They're trying to get it to rain.' Lady Serena said as the man launched another stone. The knees of his trousers were ripped, and the patches on the elbows of his shirt were falling off.

'Shall we show them how it's done?' Lady Serena said to Arthur. Before he had time to reply, she'd called to the group. 'Nimbus will make it rain.' She turned to Arthur. 'Go on.'

'Nimbus.' The word was repeated as every face swivelled towards Arthur.

'Go on,' Lady Serena urged. 'Go to the middle of them, right under the cloud.'

Arthur looked uncertainly over to Hattie before moving. He walked with hesitant steps and clenched his fists as he got closer to the group. What was about to happen? Hattie followed, stopping a few paces away from the edge of the crowd.

'Watch this,' Lady Serena called out with glee.

The group moved aside to let him through and the man with the patched clothes offered him a stone.

'He won't need that.' Lady Serena was almost purring with delight.

Halting under the cloud, Arthur looked up, waiting.

The crowd around him waited too, and Hattie took another few steps to see more.

The cloud trembled and then a small flurry of heavy raindrops appeared. A murmur went through the crowd. Then the cloud shivered again, shedding a few more drops.

'Nimbus,' Lady Serena said, and Arthur Handley-Bennett beamed.

The crowd surged towards him, taking Hattie with it. 'He made it rain,' the dishevelled woman next to Hattie shrieked. Under her dirty matted hair, her eyes were bright. Her cheeks were flushed with excitement.

Hattie was close to Arthur now, so close she could see the relief in his face. The crowd surged to be nearer to him. Fingers clasped at the sleeves of his shirt. Someone barged Hattie from behind, propelling her forwards so she was standing next to Arthur. So that she was standing under the cloud as well.

Suddenly the cloud convulsed. The rain started. Not one drop. Not ten drops. Not one hundred drops. But thousands and thousands and thousands. A torrent of big, fat, ground-soaking raindrops.

The men, women, rabbits, and pangolins lifted their faces to the sky and then together they turned to Arthur. One man hoisted him on to his bony shoulders so everyone could see him.

'Nimbus,' the crowd chanted. 'Nimbus.'

12

The rest of the journey to the Anywhere Office was like a party. The crowd who had seen the downpour followed Arthur, laughing and skipping behind him. They showed off their wet clothes to each other. They wiped their faces with their dripping sleeves. They sucked the edges of their dresses and shirts, unable to believe that it was possible for them to be so damp. And as they followed Arthur, their clothes dripped onto the dusty ground. Flowers sprang into life with every watery drop. Soon the path was covered with daisies, buttercups, crocuses, and daffodils, and every other flower Hattie had ever heard of.

But there were also some thick green shoots of a plant that Hattie didn't recognise. It never grew more than a few inches long, but Hattie noticed that whenever it got near to them, people zig-zagged or jumped out of its way. If that was what they were doing, she should probably do it too. So every time she passed a shoot, she jumped.

One zig-zag combined with a jump meant Hattie was now close to some notices that lined the path. They were covered in fine red dust — the same peppery coating that covered her boots every time her foot landed. But these were not ordinary notices. Each had the words NOTHING IS FORGOTTEN in big, bold type. And underneath, the face of a creature stared out at her. On some notices it was a hedgehog, on some a pangolin, on some a rabbit or a squirrel. On others it was a human face. Men, women, and children gazed grimly out, the only faces that weren't made happy by the passing parade.

She was staring at them, trying to decide what they meant, when a cockatoo flew past her, brushing her cheek before landing on Arthur's shoulder. It plucked a stray hair from his collar and flew back to the crowd.

'How much?' it asked as the crowd tried to snatch it from him.

'I'll give you one silve,' a man said.

'Worth more,' the cockatoo sneered.

'Two silves,' another man yelled out.

'Who give three silves?'

'I don't think I would,' a voice said in Hattie's ear as the bidding went on.

Hattie turned to see a small dragon hovering close to her shoulder. Her scales were intense purple with an iridescent sheen that flickered with different colours as it caught the light. She had the same look of intelligence as Sir Gideon and Lady Serena, but her features were gentler than either of them. The corners of her mouth curled up, not down, and the scales on her cheeks looked soft enough to stroke.

'I wouldn't take a boy's hair, even if you paid me to.' Hattie grinned at the dragon.

The corners of the dragon's mouth went up even more. 'Did you come with Sir Gideon?' she asked.

'Sort of,' Hattie told her as the dragon laughed.

'Is Sir Gideon a friend of yours?' Hattie said.

'We're in the Guild of Knight Dragons together. Lady Serena's in the Guild, too.' For a second, Hattie thought the dragon might have rolled her eyes. 'I'm Lady Violet,' the dragon continued. 'A cockatoo friend of mine called Credo told me to come because something was happening that I wouldn't want to miss.' Lady Violet flew in front of Hattie.

The purple dragon stared so deeply at Hattie it felt like she was trying to see inside her. A warmth flooded over Hattie. It was as though Lady Violet was a friend she hadn't seen for a while and who she wanted to tell everything that had happened since they'd last been together. But that was silly. Hattie had only just met her. She closed her eyes, but when she opened them again the feeling was the same. Why did she want to tell her all about home? If she wasn't careful, she'd start talking about standing on the doorstep after school each day, wondering what mood her mother would be in when she opened the door.

Just as Hattie felt that nothing would stop her from blurting out all of this, Lady Violet looked away. Her attention went to one of the notices along the side of the road, and sadness dimmed her eyes.

'Who are the pictures of?' Hattie asked.

'They're inhabitants of Somewhere-Nowhere who fought for Lord Jasper against Lord Mortimer in the Battle of the Three Volcanoes. Lord Mortimer puts the pictures here to remind everyone what will happen to them if they rise against him.'

She flew to the nearest notice and wiped the dust from the picture with her wing. 'Poor Tusker,' she muttered, as the face of a pangolin became clearer.

'What happened to him?' Hattie asked.

'He disappeared, just like all the others. Gone forever.

He was a good friend.' Lady Violet blinked hard, as though she was trying to force her sadness away, then she smiled.

'And talking of friends, I see yours,' she said.

'Who?'

'Nimbus — if that's who he is.'

'Oh, he isn't my friend,' Hattie told her. She nearly added, I don't have any friends, because they might find out about Mum. But instead she said, 'I've only just met him.'

'That doesn't mean someone isn't your friend. Look at us. We've only just met, but we're friends now.'

Hattie didn't really know what you were supposed to say when a beautiful tiny dragon said she was your friend, so she said, 'Why is Nimbus so important?'

'Because they say that when we find Nimbus the clouds will come back to Somewhere-Nowhere and it will rain again. Then there won't be so much suffering.' Lady Violet flexed her wings. 'I suppose I'd better go and look at him.' She flew to one of the notices closer to Arthur, just as the cockatoo selling Arthur's hair shouted, 'Sold for seven silves'. It took seven tiny silver coins from the man who had won the bidding and flew off to the trees with them. After a few moments, it came back without the coins and tugged another hair straight from Arthur's head.

'That hurt,' Arthur said.

'Enough,' Lady Serena shouted. 'If they want a souvenir, tell them that I'll sign whatever they want later. They can have the autograph of the knight dragon who found him.'

'Not Nimbus, but still good,' the cockatoo said and went back to tell the crowd.

Lady Serena's scales shone as brightly as the midday sun. 'Isn't it wonderful?' she said. 'Look at all those smiling people. They're so excited. They know they've seen the first miracle in the Realm in years.'

'I was called a ...' Hattie began, but Lady Serena interrupted before she could tell her that the Time Worm had called her a miracle, too.

'Of course, the Guild will want to have my portrait painted,' Lady Serena continued. 'I'll have to get my armour and shield before they do it. I expect they'll hang the painting in the Guild building. There's a space Sir Gideon's got his eye on, but I think they'll give it to me now.' She laughed. 'Perhaps I should offer everyone here an individual portrait to hang at home.' She flew to the crowd so she could tell them the idea.

'This is a bit odd,' Hattie said to Arthur as Lady Serena left.

Arthur glanced around him, to check if anyone was listening. 'It's weird. Really, really, really *weird*,' he said. 'They keep pulling my hair, calling me Nimbus, and telling me how important I am. I don't think I like it.'

'Do you know who Nimbus is?'

'Only that he's the heir to this place. And someone who can make it rain and stop the drought.' He raised his eyebrows. 'So obviously that's not me. I'm just playing along with it until I can work out how to get home.' He leaned closer to her, and for a moment his blue eyes looked wild. 'But do you know what's even weirder? It looks like I can make it rain. You saw what I did just now. You saw the downpour.' His mouth didn't quite close as he thought about what had happened. 'That was me,' he said as though he still didn't believe it.

'So do you think you're Nimbus?'

'No, I'm Arthur from Manchester.'

'But when you were standing under the cloud, you

looked like you were enjoying it. Maybe you were made to be Nimbus.'

Arthur bit his lip. 'I made sure I looked like that. Have you heard what they do to most children here?'

'Cage them,' Hattie whispered, and her mouth felt dry. That was what Sir Gideon thought should happen to her.

'This place frightens me. I want to go home,' Arthur whispered back. 'But Lady Serena would never let me, and I don't know how to do it on my own. Do you know? We could escape together.'

Hattie's chest tightened. Arthur wanted to get home, too. And maybe she did know exactly how to help him. She knew about the Time Worm. If they could find her, they might be able to persuade her to drill a hole to take them both back. And that would mean Hattie would be able to get home to her mother as well. She must have noticed that Hattie had gone by now, so who knew what state she'd be in?

But almost as soon as Hattie thought about her mother, the picture of her disappeared from Hattie's head, replaced by a picture of the red-headed girl Hattie had seen in the forest. Hattie's heart stuttered. How many more children were there in Somewhere-Nowhere like the girl, frightened and in a cage? She closed her eyes and swallowed hard. She couldn't believe what she was thinking. Her mother needed her. Of course she did. But maybe the children needed her more. She couldn't run away, knowing that they were here. She had to try to rescue them.

But that would mean she'd be choosing the children over her mother. Everything was swirling in her head. She tried to order her thoughts. And then there was Arthur. Just because she couldn't leave the children, it didn't mean Arthur had to stay, too. All Hattie had to do was tell him about the Time Worm. If he could find his way to her, he might be able to get back to Manchester. But even as she thought it, Hattie realised she didn't want that to happen. She wanted Arthur here because, in some strange way that she couldn't quite put her finger on, he made her stronger. Somehow he made her feel as though she really could rescue the red-headed girl.

She chewed the corner of her mouth. Perhaps, she told herself, she didn't need to tell Arthur about the Time Worm immediately. Perhaps it wouldn't be so bad to hold on to him for a bit longer — just until she understood a little bit more about this odd place they had both found themselves in. Then she'd let him go back. She would. She'd tell him about the Time Worm just as soon as she'd worked out how to help the red-headed girl. Really she would.

Hattie couldn't look Arthur in the eye as she replied to him.

'I've got no idea how to get home either.'

13

She'd lied to Arthur. But Hattie wasn't used to lying. She'd once thought about lying to people at school, and saying that she had a father. One who was always visiting somewhere remote to excuse him for not being there, abroad probably, doing something important like measuring the ice at the South Pole.

She'd nearly said that lie, but in the end she couldn't bring herself to do it. Yet she'd just lied so easily, for reasons she didn't quite understand. And she'd betrayed her own mother by putting a stranger before her, a girl she'd only seen for a few moments in a forest. How could she have done that? Hattie scrunched up her eyes as she imagined her mother running frantically from room to room, calling for her. 'I'm sorry,' she mouthed silently.

'Hattie, are you all right?' Arthur's voice broke through her thoughts.

'I'm sorry.' The words came out for real this time.

'Why are you sorry?'

Would he understand if she said that this place was having a strange effect on her by making her feel happy and sad at the same time? And that half of her wished Victor and Sir Gideon had thrown her back to anywhere in the human realm, but the other half wouldn't let her leave. And that she wanted to have him there with her while she worked out what was happening — at least for a while. It was tempting to tell him. Tempting, but no use. Of course he wouldn't understand, because Hattie didn't understand herself.

'Hattie? Are you okay?' Arthur asked.

Hattie focused on the freckle just by his ear so she didn't have to meet his gaze. 'I'm fine,' she said, and as she said it, she heard Lady Serena calling to Arthur. 'We need to make sure we get to the Anywhere Office before it closes.'

'Coming.' Arthur shot a look of despair at Hattie before pulling back his shoulders and transforming himself from the normal Arthur she'd just been talking to into the confident one she'd first met. 'And the weirdness starts again,' he muttered as he walked away, leaving Hattie trailing behind.

As she dawdled, she noticed a small trickle of water beside the path. It reminded her how thirsty she was. *I haven't drunk anything since I got pulled through the fridge*, she thought, wondering how there could possibly be water in a place where it didn't rain. Somewhere-Nowhere was so confusing.

Soon the flow wasn't just a trickle, and the further she walked, the wider it became, until eventually it was the size of a stream. And the bigger the stream became, the thirstier she felt.

'Drink me,' the water seemed to say as it sparkled beside her. 'Drink me now.' Thirst pinched at her mouth. It clawed at her throat. It was all she could think about. She couldn't go another step without doing something about it. She had to have a drink.

She fell to her knees and cupped her hands, ready to put them into the stream. This water seemed heavier than it was at home. It didn't flow like the water from a tap. But even though it moved so strangely, it still looked fresh and enticing.

She was about to plunge her hands into the water when a voice shouted.

'Poison!'

14

Something crashed into Hattie's cupped hands just before they touched the water. Something small and fluttering — a dragon.

'No!' Sir Gideon screamed. 'Don't drink it.' He hovered in front of her, his scales flashing a deep, anxious indigo.

'I'm thirsty,' Hattie said.

'Seeing the stream makes you thirsty, but you mustn't drink it.'

'But it looks so good. It's just some water.'

'It's poisoned.'

Hattie tried to take this in. 'So the only water you have here is poisoned?'

'It's not exactly water. It's spittle.'

'Nothing makes that much spittle.'

'The Knowledge Worm does. She runs the Anywhere Office, and this stream comes directly from there. It's one of the streams that takes the spittle away, so it doesn't flood the Anywhere Office itself.'

'The Knowledge Worm must be very dribbly.'

'She needs to be. She has to read a lot.'

'I read a lot,' Hattie said, 'and I don't dribble when I'm doing it.'

'Well, you probably don't read with your tongue,' Sir Gideon said.

Hattie just stopped herself from laughing. 'No one reads with their tongue.'

'Humans from your realm are so narrow-minded. The Knowledge Worm can read with her tongue as well as her eyes. That's how she knows if something's a lie or not. If she thinks something she's reading's not right, she licks it. She can taste lies, but they're foul and noxious, so she spits them out.' He pointed to the stream. 'All that spittle is poisoned with lies. It would kill you if you touched it.'

Hattie stared at the stream. Despite everything he'd just said, something inside her still wanted to drink it.

'Aren't you going to thank me for saving you?' Sir Gideon asked. 'A bench told me recently that you are very rude, and I'm beginning to see what it meant.'

'Is that the bench in ...?' Hattie started before she corrected herself. 'Thank you very much for saving me,' she said. And she was about to ask whether it was the bench who'd told Sir Gideon how to find her when there was a fluttering beside them.

'Sir Gideon, I didn't think you'd dare to come here,' Lady Serena purred happily.

Sir Gideon's face clouded. 'I'm going to take Hattie Brown to the Anywhere Office,' he said stiffly.

'Oh really? I thought I was doing that,' Lady Serena said.

'She's my quest.'

'I was under the impression that a child brought back from a quest had to be one of the Hundredth Children or Nimbus, not ...' Lady Serena wrinkled her nose at Hattie. '...

whatever she is. And talking of Nimbus, I don't believe you've met Arthur Handley-Bennett.'

Sir Gideon's eyes flickered as Arthur stepped forwards.

'How do you know he's Nimbus?' he asked.

'I found the Lost Seal. And then he made it rain.'

'A few drops, I'm sure. That's not enough.' Sir Gideon gave Hattie a sidelong look.

'It wasn't a few drops. It was a downpour.' Lady Serena pointed in the direction they had come. 'All those flowers have sprung from the drips of soaked clothes.'

Sir Gideon looked first at the carpet of flowers and then at Arthur Handley-Bennett. 'I never thought ...' he began.

Lady Serena laughed as she flew towards Arthur. 'So let's take Nimbus and your Hattie Brown to the Anywhere Office,' she said. 'Let's see what the Knowledge Worm has to say about not having a permit.'

'What's wrong with not having a permit?' Hattie asked Sir Gideon at the end of a long walk during which they'd followed Lady Serena, Arthur, and the joyous crowd until it stopped in front of a large turreted building made of dark stone with a squat tower at its centre.

'It means you shouldn't be here.'

'But we can ask for one at the Anywhere Office.'

Sir Gideon pointed to the building in front of them. Its windowless walls gave it a stern, brooding air, as though something secret happened inside and visitors weren't welcome. 'Does that look like the type of place you just ask for something and get it?' he said.

A cold chill crept over Hattie. The building looked more like a fortress than an office.

'And if I don't have a permit, what will they do to me?'

'Something you won't like. But I'm more worried about what they'll do to me.'

'Are we in trouble?'

For the first time, Sir Gideon almost smiled. 'Not if things work out the way I want them to. I've been busy since I last saw you.' He flew away from her and hovered at the start of a drawbridge that crossed a narrow moat and led to a wooden door studded with iron rivets.

'Is that more spittle?' Hattie asked when she reached him.

'Yes,' Sir Gideon replied. 'Whatever you do, don't fall in.'

As Hattie turned to look at the glistening liquid below them, she caught sight of the crowd who had accompanied them. None of them had followed on to the drawbridge. They had stopped on the edge of the moat and were watching them with sharp, hungry eyes. 'Aren't they coming too?' she asked.

'They can't go through the Anywhere Office into the city without a permit. They could try to get one, but they know it would never be granted, so they don't bother. Lord Mortimer only allows his supporters at the Battle of the Three Volcanoes to live inside the city. The rest have to live outside as a punishment. He never forgets who supported him and who supported The Traitor. Haven't you noticed how thin everyone is here?'

It was true. Everyone she'd met so far in Somewhere-Nowhere was as thin as a matchstick. Well, almost every-one. 'Apart from the guards,' she said.

'Exactly. And they live inside the city.' Sir Gideon tutted.

'Don't the people who live outside the city mind?'

'Of course, but there's nothing they can do about it. If they make trouble, they'll be whipped, or worse.

'Let's get on with it.' Lady Serena flew to a star-shaped

grille at the top of the great wooden door. 'We are travellers seeking permits,' she announced to whatever was on the other side.

From beyond the door, Hattie heard something that sounded like a sigh. The door appeared to open by itself. 'Enter,' a voice said from the shadows inside.

'Be very careful you don't knock anything,' Sir Gideon whispered as they walked into a large chamber filled as far as Hattie could see with higgle-piggle pillars made up of books, scrolls, parchments, pamphlets, and fragments of paper. Each seemed to go on forever, soaring up and up and up into the heart of the tower and swaying backwards and forwards like a field of corn on a windy day, always threatening to fall. Some were as tall as ladders. Some were as tall as houses. Some were as tall as steeples. All of them made Hattie want to stop and stare at the pulsing paper forest around her.

But Sir Gideon hadn't stopped. He was already following Lady Serena and Arthur, flying on a narrow route that meandered through the tottering piles towards the middle of the room. 'It didn't look this big from the outside,' Hattie said as she caught up with him.

'Knowledge is always greater than it first appears,' Sir Gideon whispered. 'Now be on your best behaviour,' he added as Hattie's gaze went up to an enormous clock that hung from the centre of the tower. Its hand stood at twenty minutes to two. Hattie frowned. It didn't feel like that should be the time, though when she thought about it, she didn't actually know what time it should feel like.

She peered round one of the swaying towers and almost squealed. Under the clock, behind a thick oak desk, loomed a gelatinous slug-like creature with a girth so big it would take eight Hatties to link arms around her. The creature's purple-green skin shimmered as she moved to one of the soaring paper pillars. Her neck reached up, narrowing like a piece of pulled putty, and she took a scrap of parchment from the pile and stared at it for a few moments. A thick tongue darted from her mouth and swept across it.

'Truth,' she declared before placing the parchment carefully behind the desk.

'She looks a bit like the Time Worm,' Hattie said.

'Cousin,' Sir Gideon whispered. 'But be careful if you mention her. Some days they're getting on, some days they're not. You never know which one it's going to be.'

The creature peered down at them with a cold stare. 'Sir Gideon and Lady Serena together again,' she observed.

'Not together,' Sir Gideon and Lady Serena both said quickly.

'We happen to be here at the same time,' Sir Gideon explained.

'I don't happen to be here,' Lady Serena snapped. 'I'm bringing Nimbus.' She paused to see the Knowledge Worm's reaction.

'Nimbus?' The Knowledge Worm looked first at Arthur and then at Hattie. 'Which one?'

'The boy, of course.' Lady Serena pointed indignantly to Arthur.

The Knowledge Worm's stare bored into Arthur Handley-Bennett. Her eyes didn't move for about a minute. Arthur shuffled first one way and then the other, as if he was keen to get away from her.

The sound of the clock ticking filled Hattie's ears, marking the seconds. Only it wasn't a proper tick. It sounded like something that was straining to move.

'Do you ...?' Arthur said after a while.

'Shhh,' the Knowledge Worm said and kept on staring,

making Hattie hope she wasn't going to do the same to her when it was her turn to be introduced.

Eventually the Knowledge Worm turned to look sternly at Lady Serena. 'So do you swear by the Code of the Knight Dragons that you'll take him straight to the palace so Lord Mortimer can prove that he's Nimbus for himself?' she asked.

'I do.'

'Then I grant the boy a permit.' The Knowledge Worm opened a drawer in a tall cylindrical cabinet and took out a piece of paper. 'Your permit,' she said as she slammed a large ornate stamp on it.

She craned her blubbery head over the desk and towards Hattie. 'And who's this?' Her lips quivered in front of Hattie as she spoke.

Hattie tried to avoid the force of the Knowledge Worm's glare. Her eyes went to the clock. Its hands were still at twenty to two, exactly the time it had said when they arrived. But if it had stopped, why could Hattie still hear the strange strain of ticking?

'I said who's this?' The Knowledge Worm's sharp voice cut into Hattie's thoughts.

Lady Serena sniggered as Sir Gideon glanced over to the door. He looked as though he was hoping something would happen.

'It's been a while since I've been here,' he said to the Knowledge Worm. 'I do believe you've laid it out a bit differently. Would you like to show us what you've done?'

The Knowledge Worm turned slowly and gazed up into the heart of the tower. She almost smiled. 'Very good, Sir Gideon, most people haven't noticed. I've adopted the new dexitaxonical system.'

'I'm always fascinated by filing,' Sir Gideon told her. 'Please tell me about it.' He glanced at the door again.

The Knowledge Worm's eyes flickered.

'I'd love to know more,' Sir Gideon insisted.

'The Knowledge Worm's mouth twisted into a half-smile. 'I would give you a full tour,' she said. 'But I see I have a human to process. Now who's this?' Her head darted quickly so Hattie had to take a step back. The papers around her separated and arched away before flexing back and regaining their shape.

Sir Gideon glanced at the door again. 'Your cousin, Marcia, sends greetings,' he said.

'But you said not to mention ...' Hattie started before Sir Gideon's wing covered her mouth.

'Marcia says she's sorry she hasn't been in touch lately,' Sir Gideon went on. 'She missed your birthday. She's very upset about it.'

'And so she should be.'

'She cried when she told me she'd missed it.'

'She cries at everything. Now who is this human girl child?'

'And have you seen Victor recently?' Sir Gideon ignored her question. 'He's getting frailer. I'm beginning to get quite worried about him.'

'Sir Gideon,' the Knowledge Worm interrupted. 'If I didn't know better I'd think you were trying to avoid the question.'

'Oh really? What question?' Sir Gideon cocked his head.

'The question about who this is.'

'Oh her,' Sir Gideon said, as if he had only just noticed Hattie. 'That's — let me see ...' His gaze darted to the door. 'Her name is Hattie Brown. Don't you think that's an ordinary name? If you had a name like Hattie Brown, wouldn't you change it?'

'Sir Gideon.'

'What Sir Gideon is trying to say is that Hattie Brown is a human-realm child who isn't one of the Hundredth Children or Nimbus,' Lady Serena said, dancing gleefully on the wooden desktop.

'Is that true, Sir Gideon?' the Knowledge Worm asked.

There were footsteps beyond the wooden door.

'No.'

'Hah!' Lady Serena said. 'You're in the wrong place for telling lies.'

'Hattie Brown is one of the Hundredth Children,' Sir Gideon said as the door to the chamber opened.

'There they are!' The guard who had arrested Hattie and Sir Gideon pointed at them as he charged into the middle of the chamber, his burgundy cloak almost tangling with the swaying paper pillars that lined his path.

'Hattie Brown is one of the Hundredth Children,' Sir Gideon said again, but in a louder voice this time. 'Why don't you ask the person who sent me on my quest?' He pointed to the guard.

'Is that you?' The Knowledge Worm loomed close to the guard, her huge face dwarfing his. The wattle that hung from her throat swung dangerously near to his eyes.

'Yes, but Hattie Brown isn't one of the Hundredth Children,' the guard said.

'Yes she is,' Sir Gideon said.

The guard looked at Sir Gideon in confusion and his mouth pulsed like a fish's.

'There's only one way of finding out,' Sir Gideon said. 'Check the ledger.'

'It won't help you.'

'Do it,' the Knowledge Worm said.

Suspiciously, the guard reached into his satchel and pulled out the ledger. He leafed through until he got to the latest entries. Slowly, he looked down a list. As he came to the bottom, his expression changed.

'But,' he said.

'What does it say?' Sir Gideon prompted.

'It says she's a Hundredth Child.' The guard blinked hard, trying to understand what was happening, and a smile crept over Sir Gideon's face. 'But she isn't, I'd have known,' the guard said.

'A Hundredth Child. Then she must have a permit.' The Knowledge Worm turned to a tall cabinet and opened a drawer.

'No!' Lady Serena's golden scales turned scarlet, and she tried to push the drawer closed with her feet.

The Knowledge Worm flicked Lady Serena aside and pulled out a permit. She put it on the desk and brought down the stamp on it. She was just about to hand it to Sir Gideon when Lady Serena called out again.

The Knowledge Worm hesitated. She snatched the ledger from the guard. Her tongue swept across the list of names.

'He's lying,' she shouted.

15

Suddenly there were hands everywhere. Grabbing hands. Clutching hands. Snatching hands. Lady Serena grabbed the ledger. The guard clutched Hattie. And Hattie snatched the permit and slipped it into her pocket.

'Lying,' the Knowledge Worm boomed into the commotion. The wattle under her throat swung back and forth like a pendulum as she swayed to and fro. 'Lying.' She heaved herself over to the spittoon and spewed saliva into the moat below.

'I've got the human girl,' the guard called out as he locked his arms further around Hattie. Then he flipped her upside-down over his back so she couldn't escape.

'Oh,' Hattie said as the blood flooded to her head. How had she got into this mess? Why hadn't she run away with Arthur when she'd had the chance?

'She's not getting away this time,' the guard growled.

'Don't hurt her!' Arthur yelled.

'She's never getting away,' Lady Serena screeched. 'She's not a Hundredth Child. She's nothing. She shouldn't be here. Arthur, come away from her, she's trouble.'

'But ...' Ignoring Lady Serena, Arthur stepped towards Hattie and the guard.

'Arthur, you are Nimbus. You can't be seen with criminals.'

'But where are they going to take her?'

'Arthur, it doesn't matter. Stay away.'

'But he can't take her.'

'I can,' the guard said. 'And I'll arrest you if you try to stop me, Nimbus or not.'

This time Arthur moved away. And while his and everyone else's attention was on Hattie and whether the guard would even flinch as her fists pummelled his back, Hattie saw Sir Gideon slip away.

Gone! Hattie couldn't believe it. Sir Gideon had abandoned her just like that. She kept on beating the guard's back as he carried her to the far end of the Knowledge Worm's chamber. Sir Gideon might have deserted her, but she wasn't going to be bundled away without a struggle. She hadn't done anything wrong.

'What's going to happen to her?' she heard Arthur ask, but the guard was moving too quickly for her to hear Lady Serena's reply. He carried her over a second drawbridge, on the side of the chamber opposite the one they'd used to enter the Anywhere Office, and marched her swiftly away.

'Where's Sir Gideon gone?' Hattie said, feeling dizzy from her upside-down view of the world. The path really shouldn't be above her head. She tried to focus on the guard's feet, but that didn't help.

'You might well ask,' the guard said. 'He flew off and left you. It looks like he's more concerned about himself than you.' A low laugh rumbled through his body, making Hattie bounce even more.

No Sir Gideon. No Victor. No Arthur. Hattie was

totally on her own. 'I'm sure he's going to find help.' She tried to sound braver than she felt. 'Where are you taking me?'

'To the city.'

'That's good, isn't it? That's where Arthur and Lady Serena are going.'

'Nimbus will never see the inside of where you're going.'

'Oh,' Hattie said, feeling even dizzier.

A wing brushed her cheek and a cockatoo tilted its head so its beak almost touched her nose.

'No point,' it said, nodding towards her pumping fists. 'Won't stop him.' Then its attention went to the top of her head. 'Bad hair.'

'I'm not really bothered about my hair at the moment,' Hattie muttered as it flew off. She tried to stop the panic that was trying to take her over. It would be most comfortable to stare at the guard's heavy feet pounding the cobbles below them, but that wasn't going to help her if she ever needed to get back to the Anywhere Office. She twisted her neck to peer around her. The guard was carrying her through a square surrounded by stone buildings with wooden doors each of which had a wreath of flowers at its centre. Spiral staircases corkscrewed on the outside of the buildings and dainty balconies were lined with more flowers. Just as Hattie was thinking that the city was prettier than she'd imagined, two hedgehogs and a squirrel scuttled in front of her. She was straining to see beyond the guard's flapping cloak to where they had gone, when he left the square and headed into an alleyway. Instantly, everything became darker. The tall buildings on either side of them didn't allow much light, even though, if Hattie twisted far enough, she could see a bright blue ribbon of cloudless sky far above her. The doors of the buildings opened straight out on to the alley and, unlike the doors in the square, they weren't festooned with flowers. It felt as though someone had put all the effort into one place and decided to ignore everything behind it.

The guard swerved into another cobbled alleyway. He turned a corner. Their route was becoming more and more confusing. Each of the alleys looked the same and, as the guard strode down yet another, Hattie realised she wouldn't have a chance of retracing their steps, even if she was looking at everything the right way up.

She shut her eyes and didn't open them again until the swaying stopped, and she pulled her head up to get a better view. They'd emerged from the labyrinth of alleyways and had halted in front of the first in a series of squat round buildings. Each of them had a single window criss-crossed with sturdy bars and a metal door that looked as though even a battering ram wouldn't budge it. As Hattie craned her head to see more, she came face-to-face with a pangolin who was squeezing past where the guard blocked its way. It stopped, looking first at her and then at the guard, before scuttling off.

'Where are we?' Hattie asked, thinking how much less nervous she'd have felt it they'd stopped outside one of the pretty buildings covered in flowers.

'You'll see soon enough.' The guard fumbled in his satchel for a key. He unlocked the door and pushed it open with a solid heave.

The door opened straight on to a set of steps, and immediately they started to descend. With every step down, Hattie's head bounced on the guard's back. She was wondering whether this was how thoughts got jumbled up when the guard hauled her from his shoulder and flung her on to a cold stone floor.

'Ouch,' Hattie said, 'that hurt.'

'It's no more than you deserve,' the guard grunted.

'Where are you going?' Hattie asked. 'You can't leave me here on my own.'

'I can and I'm going to. Goodbye.' And with that the guard turned and marched up the steps, slamming shut the door behind him when he left.

For a long time, Hattie stared up at the steps and at the door at their top without moving. Surely at any moment the guard would open it again and let her out. But soon it became clear that no one was coming. She was stuck in a dark circular room where the only light came from the barred window high above Hattie's head, making it impossible for her to see out. It was like being at the bottom of a dry well.

She must be in a prison. If everything wasn't so obviously real, she'd think this was a horrible dream. But it wasn't a dream, and she wasn't about to wake up in her bed in Worcester. She was probably as far away from Worcester and her mother as she could get. And she was probably as alone as she'd ever been. She was going to have to be careful. This was exactly the kind of situation that might start her to think bad thoughts. The kind of thoughts that felt like they belonged more to her mother, when she had The Gloom, than to Hattie.

Her eyes had become used to the light, and she stood up and went to the wall. Despite the shadows, she could just make out the outlines of the individual stones. She ran her fingers over the smooth edges, just in case there were any hidden crevices or nooks, but there was nothing. In fact, there was nothing in the room apart from a bench. At least they didn't expect her to sit on the hard floor the whole time, she thought, going to it and sitting down.

'You just don't learn, do you?' an irritated voice said.

'Is that you, Bench?'

'Of course it's me. Who do you think you're sitting on?'

'I didn't think we'd meet again.'

'Well, we did meet again. You went off without saying goodbye the last time I saw you, and you don't seem to have acquired any more manners since then.'

'I'm sorry. Would you mind very much if I sat down on you?'

'You already have, so you'd better stand up and ask again.'

For the first time since before she got to the Anywhere Office, Hattie smiled. She wasn't as alone as she'd feared. She got off the bench and took a pace back. 'Dear Bench, would you do me the honour of taking my weight?'

'That's more like it,' the bench said. 'You may sit down.'

'Thank you.' Hattie went back to where she'd been sitting. 'Why are you here?' she asked when she'd settled.

'Because of you. The guards came to the clearing and wanted to know where you'd gone.'

'And you wouldn't talk to them, so they threw you in here.' Hattie stroked the top of the bench. 'That's so kind of you, thank you.'

'Oh no, I told them exactly where you were going, but they threw me in here anyway,' the bench said grumpily.

'So you're just here because you met me and for no other reason?' That didn't seem fair.

'It seems like it.'

Hattie was about to apologise when the door at the top of the steps swung open and something tumbled down. It was big. It was heavy. It was grey.

'Ooooff,' it said as it landed at the bottom.

'Victor.' Hattie rushed over to the crumpled heap of an elephant that had just entered the room. 'Are you all right?'

Victor blinked several times, then shook his head to loosen his trunk, which had knotted in the fall. 'They didn't have to push,' he said.

Without thinking, Hattie flung her arms around him and buried her face in his neck. The beat of his heart was strong against her cheek. As she pressed closer, the anger she'd felt at him for not being there when the guard had snatched her away disappeared. She felt right in a way she couldn't explain. Right in a way that didn't come from her brain but from somewhere in the centre of her, from the part of your body that you only know is there when it's broken. 'Why are you here?' she asked.

'Oh, you know, sometimes it's good to drop in on an old friend.'

'What does that mean?'

'It means he's here because of you,' the bench said.

'Oh, hello Bench, I didn't see you there,' Victor said. 'The world's still spinning from my entrance.'

'So they arrested you because of me?' The implication of what the bench had said sank into Hattie's brain. Victor had cared about what had happened to her. 'Did they come and hunt you down?' she asked.

'More like I thought I'd better come and find you,' Victor said.

So Victor didn't just care, he cared enough to get himself into trouble. Hattie took in a long breath as Victor looked around. 'I don't think much of the accommodation they've given us,' he said.

'Where do you think this is?'

'It's one of Lord Mortimer's cells. And not the best one by the look of it.'

'What will they do with us?'

Victor didn't answer immediately. 'That depends,' he said eventually.

'That depends on whether Lord Mortimer wants you to die in pain or not,' the bench said before Victor could finish.

'Quiet.' Victor's trunk slapped the top of the bench.

'I'm only telling the truth.'

'Why would Lord Mortimer want me to die in pain?' Hattie asked. It didn't make sense. She was just a girl from Worcester who lived alone with her mother and went to a school where she'd made sure that no one beyond her class-mates would know her name.

'As an example of what happens to someone who comes to Somewhere-Nowhere without permission,' Victor told her, looking serious. 'He's frightened that there will be an uprising in support of his brother, and he thinks scaring people's the way to make sure that doesn't happen.'

'I thought he beat his brother already.'

'He did but some people think Lord Jasper should still be the ruler here.'

'Why? Is he older?'

'No, Lord Mortimer is a year older than Lord Jasper.'

Hattie frowned. 'So what's the fuss about? Surely that means Lord Mortimer is automatically the ruler.'

'That's not how it's done here,' Victor told her. He shifted his weight to make himself more comfortable. 'Any one of a ruler's children can become their heir. The next ruler is chosen through a test when the child is around eleven or twelve. But they don't know what that test is, and it changes every generation. It's written in The Book of the

Realm, which is locked in a chamber deep within the Knowledge Worm's library. The chamber is only opened when the Book of the Realm is ready. That means no one can know how they're being tested, so they can't cheat by pretending to be one kind of person when really they're another.

'Sometimes the test is a feat of courage, like fighting a battle. Sometimes it's an act of kindness, like helping a beggar. Lord Mortimer and Lord Jasper's test was how they treated the Time Worm. Ever since he was a young boy, Lord Mortimer had taunted her for crying. He'd thrown sticks and rocks at her and set traps for her to fall into. Lord Jasper had always been kind to her. So, despite the fact Lord Mortimer was a great swordsman and warrior, Lord Jasper became Nimbus. And, when his mother died, he became ruler.'

'Until he married someone from your realm,' the bench interrupted.

'That was Lord Mortimer's opportunity,' Victor said. 'He told everyone how Lord Jasper was a threat to the whole of Somewhere-Nowhere. He made them believe that Lord Jasper was plotting with the humans from your realm to make us slaves. And many inhabitants of Somewhere-Nowhere believed him. He raised an army against Lord Jasper. And when he won, Lord Mortimer punished everyone who fought against him. Some just disappeared. The rest were banned from the city.'

'Did you support Lord Mortimer?' Hattie asked.

Victor's ears flattened against the sides of his head and he glanced away from her. 'I didn't fight for him, but I did nothing to stop him either. Sometimes that's all it takes for bad things to happen. It was before I realised what Lord Mortimer was truly like. I thought that maybe he was right about the humans. But now I wish I could go back and do things differently.'

'So you think humans like me would destroy Some-where-Nowhere?'

'I thought that once, but not now. Now I think only some would do that.'

Hattie tried to make sense of what she was hearing. 'But if Lord Mortimer punished everyone, wouldn't he punish the Time Worm? He must hate her for being the test he failed.'

'He'd like to, but he needs her too much.'

'She steals the clouds,' the bench added.

Victor nodded. 'After the Battle of the Three Volcanoes, the clouds left,' he said. 'They went to the remotest parts of Somewhere-Nowhere, and every time anyone went near, they moved away. Everyone believes they went in protest because the true heir to Somewhere-Nowhere had been overthrown. It means the Time Worm is our only way of getting clouds and rain. So Lord Mortimer might love to get his revenge on her, but he can't.'

'And because of all this, Lord Mortimer might kill me.' Hattie was in more danger than she'd been in her life, and for something she hadn't done.

Victor shifted his position, and Hattie couldn't feel the beat of his heart anymore. 'That's not necessarily what will happen,' he told her. 'I just need to think things through to make sure it doesn't.'

'But if you don't think things through the right way, I could die.' Hattie heard how tight and scared her voice sounded. 'But you'll stop that happening, won't you?' The knot in her stomach, which had disappeared when she saw Victor, had returned. 'Arthur gets to be Nimbus, and I get to die. That's not fair. What makes Arthur so special?'

'He can make it rain,' Victor said.

'I can make it rain.'

'Just a few drops.'

'That's all Arthur can do,' Hattie said.

'According to the cockatoos, Arthur made it pour. And anyone who makes it pour is special round here.'

'But it only poured when I —'

'I'm feeling very strange from my tumble,' Victor interrupted. 'Would it be a great inconvenience if I rested for a few moments on your back?' he said to the bench. 'I would be most obliged.'

'I suppose so.' The bench sounded quite put out.

Victor sat down heavily, then he shuffled as though he was finding the comfiest spot.

'My bottom's blocking his ears,' he whispered to Hattie. 'Now what were you about to say about the downpour?'

'When Arthur was trying to make it rain on his own, he only got a small shower. The downpour happened when I walked under the cloud.'

Victor's eyes flashed excitedly and, for the first time since he'd pulled her through the fridge, he stopped looking tired.

'Victor,' Hattie said, a flutter starting in her chest. 'Does that mean I'm Nimbus, not Arthur?'

Victor closed his eyes slowly. He took three deep breaths. When he opened his eyes again, the excitement was gone. 'No, Hattie,' he said. 'It doesn't mean anything. And you should be careful what you wish for.'

16

Outside in the city, away from where Hattie, Victor and Bench sat at the bottom of a deep, miserable cell, word had spread that Nimbus had arrived. Makeshift stalls selling candyfloss, marshmallows, and crackle toffee sprang up along the cobbled road. Fairy lights twinkled in the trees. A band called Nimbus played a jig. Children clutched balloons with Arthur's name on them. Artists sketched portraits of him. And the crowds kept coming from every corner of the city. Parents carried their children on their shoulders. Families of rabbits, hedgehogs, and squirrels skipped and danced with each other. Long-snouted pangolins gazed longingly from just outside the group. They celebrated in different ways, but they were all there for the same thing. They came for Arthur Handley-Bennett. They came for Nimbus.

'This is all for us,' Lady Serena told Arthur as she flew alongside him.

Her words brought Arthur's attention back from worrying about Hattie. He frowned at Lady Serena. She was beautiful, like a golden goddess at his side, but what would happen when she worked out that he was just plain Arthur from Manchester, not Nimbus after all? Would she get a guard to grab him, just like Hattie? Probably. Whatever she pretended, Arthur could see that Lady Serena's eyes were distant because she cared for who she thought he was, not for who he knew he was. But his fate had somehow become wrapped up with hers, so he'd better play along. Pulling all his worries into a smile so tight it hurt his cheeks, Arthur waved at the crowd. He turned first one way and then the other, making sure he gave each side equal time so that no one could complain that Nimbus hadn't given them enough attention. Each time he waved in their direction, the crowd cheered, as though he was a conductor playing an orchestra. If he didn't feel so uneasy, it would be funny.

'Lady Serena, can I ask you something?' he said.

'Of course.' Lady Serena bowed towards a young girl, who was holding a banner decorated with golden flowers.

'How can I be Lord Mortimer's heir when I've never met him?'

'Lord Mortimer doesn't have a wife or children. If something happens to him, the Realm will go to ...' Lady Serena checked over her shoulder to see if anyone could hear them. 'Lord Mortimer's brother, Lord Jasper,' she whispered when she was sure they weren't being overheard.

'What's wrong with that?'

'Everything,' she said, shuddering. 'We'd probably be dead or slaves if he was still ruling us. We're so lucky Lord Mortimer fought against him.' She closed her eyes and her golden scales dimmed. 'We lost so many of the Guild in the battle, but we won in the end. The memory of the fallen is honoured by our victory.'

'What's that got to do with me?' Arthur asked.

'Lord Jasper and his human-realm wife had a child. A boy. They say that when the uprising started, Lord Jasper sent his wife, the child, and the Lost Seal to the human realm to protect them. No one knows where. That's why the knight dragons go on quests to the human realm. They're looking for the child and the Lost Seal.' Lady Serena's scales glowed even more intensely. 'And I was the dragon who succeeded.'

Arthur tried to take in what that meant. 'So you think I'm that child? Lord Mortimer's nephew? But my dad's called Martin. He isn't a lord.'

'The man you call father isn't Lord Jasper. Lord Jasper's in a prison away from here, near the volcanoes,' Lady Serena said. 'Don't frown,' she added. 'People might think something's wrong.'

'Of course I'm going to frown. You're saying my dad's not my dad!'

'Exactly,' Lady Serena said breezily.

'But if Lord Mortimer doesn't like Lord Jasper, why would he want his son as his heir?'

'Because when we find Nimbus, the clouds will return and the rain will come. And no one will have any reason to say that the drought is to punish us for what happened to Lord Jasper. And then Lord Mortimer's enemies will finally stop plotting against him. Oh look,' Lady Serena said, 'they're sketching us. I think I'll wear green for this one.' Her wings changed colour as she landed on Arthur's shoulder to pose.

'And what about Hattie?' Arthur asked. 'What will happen to her?'

'Don't worry about her.'

'But she seemed nice, and they arrested her for nothing. Where did they take her?'

'To the city cells, I expect.' Lady Serena put out her wings and tilted her head. 'This is my best side,' she called to the artist.

'But Hattie hasn't done anything.' Arthur couldn't believe she didn't care. He chewed the side of his lip. He wished he was back in Manchester. Everything was so much simpler there. In Manchester his dad was really his dad. At least he acted like his dad should. He did what everyone's dad did. He was a bit cross sometimes and a bit forgetful at other times. But mostly he was okay, with bad taste in music and worse taste in jokes. That was who Arthur had always thought his dad was, not some strange lord who'd been locked up by his brother.

Arthur felt his forehead tighten. He used to think he liked adventures. But now it seemed he liked them when they were on a computer screen. Why couldn't all this weirdness be happening on a screen in his bedroom? Why did it have to be real?

'But if you don't want the humans to know you're here, why do you bring the Hundredth Children through?' he asked.

Now it was Lady Serena's turn to frown. 'They're necessary,' she said after a while.

'And I came without a permit.'

'But you're Nimbus. Nimbus doesn't need a permit.'

Arthur wished he wasn't Nimbus. He hadn't asked to be Nimbus, and he didn't like being Nimbus. He could think of a hundred people in his school who'd jump at the chance to be really important like this. People who wouldn't mind being told that their dad wasn't their dad. Let them do it.

'Do you want to know how I know you're Nimbus?' Lady Serena asked. 'I found something in your house.'

Two cockatoos swooped towards them holding a garland made of yellow and white flowers. They draped it around Arthur's neck just as he was asking, 'What did you find?'

Lady Serena looked up from where she was signing autographs. 'The Lost Seal,' she said.

17

A line of elephants stood by the side of the road as Arthur and Lady Serena continued their route through the city. Their trunks were raised, and they bellowed triumphantly as Arthur and the dancing crowd around him passed. He'd never seen a real live elephant before, and suddenly he'd seen loads, and they all seem to be here for him.

They turned the corner and the crowd spilled out in front of an imposing building that filled one side of a large cobbled square. Its stone walls were lighter than any of the other buildings he'd seen in the city, a warm honey colour, which extended to the steps that invited visitors to approach its wide portico entrance. But the windows were the most eye-catching thing about what was in front of him. On the building's first storey they were star-shaped, on its second storey arched, and on its third storey round. And as Arthur's gaze moved up to the turreted roof, a guard whispered something in Lady Serena's ear.

'That's good,' she said before turning to Arthur. 'We're going straight into the palace. Let's look at you.' She fussed at the garland around his neck, plucking out an untidy leaf. 'Let's take you to Lord Mortimer. There's no point in hanging around.'

Three dragons flew over and draped a cloak around Lady Serena's shoulders, while the elephants who had accompanied them to the square trumpeted another tuneless chorus as Arthur followed Lady Serena to the doors of the palace. When the trumpeting had finished, the doors swung open, revealing a hallway and a further set of doors, even taller and wider than the first. Two guards eased the doors open, letting them into a room larger than any Arthur had seen before. Above him was a ceiling of soaring arched beams, each one decorated with animals. Carved dragons, elephants, and pangolins peered down, making him feel like he was being spied on. Wooden geckos, baboons, and monkeys scaled every column, as if trying to see him better. Wooden hedgehogs, squirrels, and piglets huddled at each base, gazing at him from below.

At the far end of the hall, raised on a dais and silhouetted against the light coming through three star-shaped windows, Arthur saw a thin figure with jet-black hair hunched over a chess board. In profile his nose looked perfectly straight. Its sharp tip pointed at the chess pieces in front of him.

The figure looked up as they entered. Now Arthur could see that his pale skin was like polished marble and far smoother than anyone else's he'd met in Somewhere-Nowhere. He held the white queen from the chess set in his long fingers, squeezing her crown. 'Lady Serena.' A voice as smooth as chocolate filled the hall.

Lady Serena bowed. 'Lord Mortimer.'

'I hear you've brought me something.' Lord Mortimer

stood up, and Arthur realised he was much, much taller than he'd at first appeared.

'Bring him forward,' Lord Mortimer pointed his slender finger as though he was aiming a weapon at Arthur's heart.

'Go on,' Lady Serena said.

'Go where?' Arthur thought he'd prefer not to go any closer to Lord Mortimer. There was something about him that made him want to turn and leave this strange over-elaborate hall that very moment.

'Into the light. Let him see you.' Lady Serena's scales pulsed silver, then returned to gold.

Arthur stepped forwards, passing a long line of courtiers. Men, women, rabbits, squirrels, hedgehogs, and pangolins gazed at him in awe. He felt his face going red. No one had looked at him like this before. Not even his mother when he'd won the science prize at school.

'Closer,' Lord Mortimer said. 'I want to see you properly.'

Arthur stopped in front of him. Without saying a word, Lord Mortimer stared and stared and stared. Then he prowled around him, without dropping the stare for a moment. *Stop*, Arthur thought. *Please stop*. He felt like he was an exhibit in a museum. And not one Lord Mortimer liked much.

But Lord Mortimer didn't stop until he'd gone full circle.

'Hello, I'm Arthur,' Arthur said at last, hoping that this would make Lord Mortimer look at him normally again. 'I'm very pleased to meet you,' he added, because that's what he thought his father would have told him to do — or the man he'd thought of as his father until not long ago. But instead of sounding pleased, his voice sounded nervous.

Lord Mortimer didn't respond. He just continued to

stare. His eyes were so black that the light wasn't reflected in them at all. And although Arthur wanted to look away and break the spell between them, he didn't dare. It felt as though that look between him and Lord Mortimer was the only thing that was keeping everything in the world together.

Suddenly, Lord Mortimer turned and put the chess piece he was still holding back on the board. 'Checkmate,' he said, knocking the black king over before his attention swung back to Arthur. 'Have they been treating you well?'

'Yes,' Arthur replied. But that didn't sound enough for a man who'd made him feel this uneasy, so he added, 'Like royalty.'

'If Lady Serena's right, that's what you are,' Lord Mortimer said. 'Where are you from, Arthur?'

'Manchester.'

'Manchester?' Lord Mortimer rolled the word around his mouth as though he was about to eat it. 'So that's where you were. We've been looking for you so hard and you were in Manchester all the time.' He let out a throaty laugh. Immediately, Lady Serena laughed. And then the guard laughed. Then everyone in the hall joined in. 'Manchester.' The sound went through the crowd. 'Manchester.' It was as if it was the funniest joke they'd ever heard.

Arthur felt his throat go dry. Was he supposed to laugh, too? Was Manchester really this funny? He was the only one who hadn't thought it hilarious. It must be safest to join in. 'Manchester,' he roared, without knowing what he was laughing about.

'Quiet!' Lord Mortimer yelled. And instantly the whole room snapped into silence, including Arthur. All apart from a pangolin, who kept sniggering. Everyone around him turned and looked at him in horror.

'Seize him!' Lord Mortimer yelled.

The pangolin rolled into a ball, but a guard rushed forward and grabbed his tail, flinging him against a pillar. There was a sickening sound as a line of scales on his left-hand side cracked.

'No!' Arthur cried as the pangolin yelped.

'It's no more than he deserves for not obeying me immediately,' Lord Mortimer said.

The guard pulled back his arm to throw the pangolin against the pillar a second time, but just as the downward thrust was about to come, Lord Mortimer held up his hand. 'Not now,' he said. 'Take him to one of the cells.'

'Your Lordship.' The guard nodded and rolled the balled pangolin along the floor in front of him with his staff.

'But ...' Arthur started, before he saw Lady Serena shaking her head at him furiously. He clamped his mouth shut and thought of Hattie. She was in one of Lord Mortimer's cells. And if this was what he did to someone who laughed at the wrong time, she was in trouble.

Lord Mortimer's black eyes locked on Arthur again. 'Who were you with in Manchester?' he demanded.

'My mother and my ...' Arthur hesitated. 'My father,' he added. It sounded odd saying it after what Lady Serena had told him.

'Describe them.'

'My mother is a nurse and my ... my father works in insurance.' He wished so badly he could get back to them.

'And what do they look like?'

'My father is short-sighted and looks a bit like an owl.'

'And your mother?' Lord Mortimer looked particularly keen to know.

'My mother has red hair and freckles.'

Lord Mortimer scowled. 'Do you get your curly hair from her?'

'No, her hair's straight.' Arthur wished he could leave but Lord Mortimer was firing questions at him like bullets.

'And what colour are her eyes?'

'Brown.'

'You're sure?'

'Yes.'

'And how tall?'

'About the same height as my father. I'm the tall one in our family.' Why was he bothering to tell Lord Mortimer about his father? He seemed more interested in his mother. Arthur wished Lord Mortimer's questions would stop.

But they kept coming. 'Do you have a picture of her?' Lord Mortimer demanded.

'No.'

Lord Mortimer sighed. 'I see,' he said. 'We should let you get settled in. There will be plenty of time to talk when you've freshened up. I'm being a bad host. Is there anything I can do for you?'

Arthur thought about begging him to let him go home, but he was pretty certain that wasn't what Lord Mortimer meant. The easiest thing would be to say nothing and get away from Lord Mortimer's unnerving stare, but there was something he needed to do, even if it made Lord Mortimer angry again.

He screwed up all of his courage and took a deep breath. 'Actually,' he said. 'There is one thing.'

18

Hattie watched Victor as he extended his trunk to try to reach the window of the cell. 'It's too far,' he told her and Bench. 'We're definitely not getting out that way.'

'I could sing to keep our spirits up,' Bench told them. And before Victor and Hattie could say anything, he started to hum. Soon the hum became louder, until eventually he started a rousing tune in a rasping, gruff voice.

'I would ask you to stop, but it's surprisingly comforting,' Victor said.

'You could join in,' Bench told them between tunes.

But neither of them did.

After a while, Hattie decided that the bench's voice wasn't grating after all. Perhaps it was soothing enough to help her go to sleep, even though it wasn't dark. In fact, the light hadn't changed all the time she'd been in Somewhere-Nowhere, she thought as she lay down on the bench and pulled her clothes tightly around her. As her eyelids became heavier, the bench's voice seemed to soften, and the last thing she remembered seeing before she fell asleep were Victor's soulful eyes watching her.

The next thing Hattie knew, something woke her. For a few seconds, she thought she was in her bedroom in Worcester. *I'd better make sure Mum is okay to get up*, she thought. And then she remembered. She was in a place far away from Worcester. And far away from where she could make sure her mother didn't stay in bed all day and miss her shift at work. And she was in a lot of trouble.

She rubbed her eyes and looked around. Standing with his back pressed hard against the wall of their cell, Victor didn't seem to have moved. It was as if he'd been watching over her all the time she'd been asleep. Hattie swallowed hard. This was what she did when her mother was really bad. But no one had ever done it for her before.

Seeing her gazing at him, Victor smiled. 'Hello, Hattie.' His voice sounded soft and warm, as though he really was pleased to see her.

'Hello, Victor. Hello, Bench. Is it morning?'

The happiness disappeared from Victor's face. 'We don't really have mornings any more,' he said. 'Not since the clock stopped after the Battle of the Three Volcanoes.'

'One clock stopping doesn't mean mornings don't happen.'

'It does when the clock is in the Anywhere Office.'

Hattie's mind went to the enormous clock she'd seen hanging from the centre of the Anywhere Office's tower. Its hands had been at twenty minutes to two when she'd arrived, and they were still in exactly the same place when she'd left. 'But time just can't stand still,' she said, not wanting to believe. 'It just can't.'

'The Battle of the Three Volcanoes tore the heart out of Somewhere-Nowhere. Lots of things we thought were impossible happened after that,' Victor told her.

'Like the clouds leaving,' the bench said, and Hattie felt

him shift beneath her. 'But I haven't asked. Did you sleep well?' he added.

Hattie and Victor exchanged glances. 'Thank you for letting me lie on you,' Hattie said.

She felt the bench shift some more. 'I tried to be as soft as possible, but you were very wriggly.'

'Sorry — I didn't mean to be.' Hattie stroked the top of the bench and looked back at Victor. 'Do you think we can get out?' she asked.

The bench snorted. 'Chance would be a fine thing.'

'If this was a film one of us would pretend to be sick and we'd overpower the guard when he came to investigate,' Hattie said.

Victor looked sceptical. 'Do they really fall for that?'

'They do in the films.'

'I suppose we've got nothing to lose. Let's try it.'

So Hattie clutched her stomach and began to moan. She moaned as if she were a ghost who had been dead for a thousand years. But no one came to the door.

'Maybe the guard can't hear you,' Victor said.

So Hattie cried as though she were a baby who hadn't been fed for a week.

'Ouch,' the bench said. 'That hurt my ears.'

But no one came to the door.

'Maybe the guard doesn't like babies,' the bench said.

So Hattie howled like a pack of wolves that hadn't eaten for a million years.

This time the door at the top of the steps opened and the guard's face peered down at them.

'I'm hurt. I'm hurt,' Hattie yelled, throwing herself on to the ground.

'What happened?'

'The elephant kicked me.'

'Victor would never kick anyone.'

'He did it by accident.'

The guard moved, and Victor tried to make himself very flat, as though he wasn't a great big elephant who liked butter. His trunk inched towards the leg of the bench so he could snatch it up as a weapon when the guard came down.

'Really?' the bench said, wearily, as Victor tightened his grip.

At the sound of his voice, the guard froze. He looked down the steps, then started to laugh. 'Is the human-realm child doing the thing where someone pretends to be ill so you can pounce on me?' he asked, his belly wobbling as his laughter grew.

'He really did kick me,' Hattie protested.

'No, he didn't. I've told you that Victor wouldn't ever hurt you,' the guard said. 'I should have realised that it was a lie immediately. What a joke.'

He was just laughing some more when a scraping sound made him stop. He turned to see what it was, and his face was overcome with a look of pure astonishment. The look was still on his face as he moved aside to let someone pass. And as he did so, Hattie, Victor, and the bench saw who it was at the top of the steps.

Arthur smiled nervously. 'Hello, Hattie. I've come to set you free.'

19

Hattie walked from the cell flanked by Victor and Arthur. Lady Serena fluttered beside Arthur and, behind them all, walked the guard, nodding to anyone who saw them, keen to make sure that they were aware of the company he was keeping. This was the first time Hattie had seen the inside of the city when she wasn't slung over the shoulder of a guard, kicking and screaming like she was a little child again. Now it was the right way up, the first thing she thought was how clean the city was. The red dust that coated everything outside didn't seem to exist here.

A cheer greeted them as they emerged into a square lined with buildings decked with flowers. 'It's him. It's Nimbus,' a hedgehog squealed, and Hattie saw Arthur look down to the ground, blushing. The crowd before them was about the same size as the one that had accompanied them to the Anywhere Office, but that was where the similarities ended. These rabbits were plump, their fur glossy, not matted and patchy. The squirrels' tails were bushy, not tatty. The hedgehogs' quills were sharp, not broken. And the people wore smart clothes, not rags. Hattie took in every difference. So not everyone in Somewhere-Nowhere was desperate. Lord Mortimer must hate everyone who lived outside the city if he didn't want them to be as healthy as everyone she saw around her.

But thinking this didn't spoil her happiness at being freed quite as much as she might have expected. And the two reasons for that were walking beside her. She glanced first at Arthur and then at Victor, stretching out her hand to touch his hide. She would have put her hand out to touch Arthur, too, apart from the fact it would have been what he'd call 'weird'. So she just smiled at him instead. Only Sir Gideon hadn't been there when she'd needed him. He'd run away the moment there was trouble. She didn't know where the cowardly dragon was now, but she knew she was well rid of him.

A call of 'Make it rain, make it rain' pulled Hattie's attention back to the crowd. A woman with a swirling green cloak was calling out to Arthur. Hattie watched him smile uncertainly, then look up. 'There aren't any clouds.' He sounded relieved.

The woman wasn't put off. 'Go to the Keep,' she called after him. 'Make it rain.'

Arthur kept walking, smiling nervously.

'Go to the Keep,' the woman called again.

Beside her, a man nodded. 'Go to the Keep,' he joined in.

The idea spread. First it was a murmuring, then it grew louder. Soon the whole of the crowd was chanting. 'The Keep, the Keep. Go to the Keep.'

'But I don't know where the Keep is,' Arthur said, his smile growing tenser.

'It's over there, just outside the city.' Lady Serena

pointed away from where they were going, but her eyes stayed nervously on the crowd.

'Why do they want us to go there?' Arthur asked.

'It's where they keep the clouds before the Hundredth ...' Her voice faltered, but she recovered her composure quickly. 'I think we should go back to Lord Mortimer,' she said briskly. 'That way.' She pointed in the opposite direction.

Before Arthur could move, a young boy stood in front of him. A balloon with Arthur's grinning face on it bobbed menacingly above them both. 'Go to the Keep,' the boy said. Twenty people swarmed round Arthur.

Lady Serena's scales turned mauve. Hattie wondered what the problem was. She glanced over to Victor. He was watching what was going on intently.

'Go to the Keep,' the crowd urged. 'Make it rain. Go to the Keep.'

'We need to go to see Lord Mortimer.' Lady Serena's voice was strained.

Hattie saw Victor's back arch, as if he was about to say something.

'Go to the Keep.'

'No,' Lady Serena said, her wings fluttering anxiously.

'I think I'd better do it,' Arthur told her, eyeing the crowd around them. 'They're not going to stop until I do. I'll go to the Keep,' he announced, and the crowd cheered. They began to surround him, pushing him along with them, away from the path that would take them to Lord Mortimer.

I hope the thing that's making Lady Serena so flustered isn't a problem, Hattie thought as the crowd swept him away.

20

The crowd propelled Arthur further away from Hattie as the march to the Keep began. They swarmed to a gate in the wall. The guard on duty was so excited to see Nimbus that he hardly glanced at the permit Hattie had snatched in the kerfuffle at the Anywhere Office. With a nod of his head, she found herself back in the parched rusty-red landscape of the world outside the city. Another guard led the parade, striding ahead of the throng. He held his staff high in the air until they reached a tall tower that soared into the cloudless sky. He rapped importantly on the door. A man stuck his head out of a window and looked with disapproval at the commotion below.

'Who's that?' Hattie asked Victor as they hung back, away from the crowd.

'The Cloud Keeper,' Victor replied.

Who would believe that was a job? Hattie thought as the guard bellowed, 'Nimbus has come to make rain from one of the clouds.'

The Cloud Keeper stared in amazement at Arthur

before bowing his head. 'I shall do whatever Nimbus wishes.'

Soon Hattie heard heavy footsteps as the hobnailed boots of a human figure climbed the stone staircase that snaked around the outside of the tower. Eventually, the Cloud Keeper reached the top, puffing as he caught his breath. He braced himself and positioned a broad shoulder behind something round, shoving and straining with the full weight of his body until an opening appeared in the top of the tower. A small wispy cloud sprang out of the gap.

The crowd cheered as it bounced up into the sky. 'Make it rain.' They surged forward, taking Arthur with them, jostling each other to stand under the cloud. Every man, woman, and child turned towards Arthur. Every pangolin, every rabbit, every cockatoo.

'Make it rain,' they chanted. 'Make it rain.'

Arthur smiled, and Hattie wondered how he could look so confident. No one else would suspect that wasn't how he felt. She wished she was that good at disguising her feelings.

Arthur turned his face up to the skies. He raised up his arms.

'Make it rain.'

Above Arthur, Hattie saw the cloud stop. It shivered then a small shower of rain fell.

'Rain!' the crowd roared. 'More! More!'

Arthur looked up again. The cloud shivered again. Fresh drops blossomed and fell.

'More! More! More!' the crowd shouted as each one emerged.

But no more drops came. Every face turned to Arthur. He raised his arms again but the cloud did nothing.

'Make it rain,' the crowd demanded.

Hattie felt her chest tighten as Arthur stretched higher.

She shot a look to Victor. He'd told her that she hadn't helped Arthur make it pour the first time. So why was she worried about him being able to make it pour on his own now?

'Make it rain,' the crowd ordered, but the cloud didn't do anything.

She couldn't bear it anymore. 'I'm going to go to Arthur,' she whispered to Victor.

'No.' Victor's voice was sharp.

'More! More!' the crowd chanted. For the first time, Arthur looked nervous. His hands quivered uncertainly as he gazed at the cloud above him.

'He needs me,' Hattie hissed.

'You mustn't bring attention to yourself.' Victor's weight shifted as if he was about to try to block her way. *No*, Hattie thought. *You can't stop me. My friend's in trouble. You can't stop me helping him.*

She dived away from Victor, lunging towards the centre of the crowd, towards where Arthur stood. She ran under the cloud.

As she moved, the cloud above her convulsed, and suddenly raindrops drenched the crowd. 'Nimbus, Nimbus,' they cried, tipping their faces to the rain. And as they fell to their knees, Hattie felt something swoosh behind her. Victor's trunk circled her waist as he snatched Hattie from under the cloud. Away from the crowd. Away from Arthur. Away from Nimbus.

21

Hattie flew through the damp air, carried by Victor, before he placed her on the ground, far from the crowd.

'There was no need to snatch me away,' she snapped, brushing the water off her face and rearranging her neck-lace. Behind Victor, she could see the faces of the crowd. Some had let their mouths hang slack so the drops could fall straight on to their tongues. Others had cupped their hands and were lapping like dogs at the water pooling in their palms. As flowers sprang to life at their feet, mothers picked them and wove them into their children's hair. While she'd been flying through the air, she'd even heard one mother tell her son to watch and to remember, so he could always recall every detail of the day Nimbus had made it rain.

'There was every need to snatch you away,' Victor said.

'I was doing a good thing. I was making it rain.'

Victor looked as though he was waiting for her to correct herself and say it was Arthur, not her. But she knew what had happened. She wasn't going to lie just to please him.

'*I* made it rain, *not* Arthur,' she hissed.

'No, Arthur made it rain.' His voice was gentle, but firm.

'A small shower. It wasn't going to do anything more than that until I ran under the cloud.'

'You're misinterpreting what happened.'

'I know what I did, and I know what happened. Before I moved there was a bit of a shower, and after I moved everyone got soaked. So don't tell me that Arthur made it rain, not me.'

'I heard that you tried to make a cloud rain when you were in the forest,' Victor said. 'How much rain did you manage then? I believe it was just a small shower.'

How did he know about that? The surprise almost made her stumble, but something inside her wanted to keep on fighting. 'That's more than you can do,' she said.

'Perhaps,' Victor replied in the low voice that made him sound like an adult who knows they are going to win an argument whatever the other person says. 'But any other human-realm child can do what you can do.'

'I thought —' Hattie started.

'You and Arthur are both human-realm children. You can both make a little rain. Have you met any other human-realm children here?'

'Not really.' Hattie thought about the girl with the red hair, but they hadn't really met.

'Well, if you did, they'd be able to make a small shower, too.'

'Oh.' That was puzzling. 'But what you've just said doesn't explain the downpour. It wasn't just a bit of rain when I went under the cloud. It was pouring.'

Victor looked at Hattie disapprovingly. 'You're making it sound like you're Nimbus,' he said.

Hattie was beginning to wonder if Victor was playing with her. 'Maybe I am.' She pulled back her shoulders as she said it. Everyone might be saying that Nimbus was a boy, but it looked as though this boy needed a girl. She'd had enough of people dismissing her at home. She wasn't going to let that happen here. 'I made it rain.'

'Hattie Brown, you are not Nimbus.'

'Then why didn't you let me go home? Why did you stop me going back to Mum? She needs me.' Her head was pounding. She glanced at the crowd in the distance that was still celebrating with Arthur. She didn't want everyone to be crowding around her like they were around him, telling her she was special, but she didn't like being ignored either. She should have told Arthur she knew of a way back to the human realm when he'd asked her. They might have been back home by now. They might be in a place where everything wasn't '*weird*'. She felt her legs longing to run. Why not? It would give her a chance to think straight. She started to move.

She sprinted away from Victor and away from where the crowd was still surrounding Arthur. She found herself running along the side of a high wall that led away from the Keep. It stretched ahead, towering over her, making it impossible to see what was on the other side. Her breath was already short when she reached a corner. She sprinted round it — and stopped dead.

She was beside bars, not a wall. And behind those bars were children. Hundreds and hundreds of children. All of them about eleven or twelve. All of them staring at her in silence. Her heart stuttered. It shouldn't be possible for so many children to be this quiet.

But before she had time to take in more, something had wrapped itself around her waist. For a few seconds, she seemed to be flying through the air, until she realised Victor had picked her up and tucked her in front of him. He was pounding back down the side of the high brick wall, towards where they'd been before.

When he got there, he set her down. 'Who were they?' Hattie gasped for air. 'Are they from my world?'

Victor raised his head slowly. The wrinkles on his face were like deep valleys and his eyes were sad. 'I'm sorry you saw that,' he said.

'There are boys and girls in a cage! People like me in a prison!' She couldn't believe he wasn't as angry as she was. 'Who are they?'

Victor's eyes became dense with sorrow. 'Those are the Hundredth Children. Lord Mortimer tells the knight dragons to bring back a child from every hundredth house they visit in your realm. They stay here for a while, and then they are returned to the human realm and others take their place. It saddens me to say that Somewhere-Nowhere needs them.' He looked up as something whooshed in from above them. A cockatoo landed on Hattie's shoulder and pressed its beak to her ear. 'Go. Nimbus now,' it urged.

'But there's something Victor and I need to talk about.'

'To Nimbus.' The cockatoo was insistent.

Hattie started to move, but that didn't mean she was going to forget about the children. She'd find out what was happening to them, whether Victor liked it or not. She glanced in the direction of the crowd. At its centre, Arthur was waiting for her. Even from a distance Hattie could see that he was trying to smile. That smile would disappear pretty quickly if he'd seen what she'd seen. His stomach would cramp with sickness, just like hers.

'Wait,' the cockatoo said. 'Hair mess.' It fussed around her head, moving forwards and back to check its work before it was satisfied. 'To Nimbus,' it said at last.

The crowd was still chanting as she neared them. 'Nimbus,' they were saying. Their voices got louder with every step she took. 'Nimbus.'

'Hattie.' The moment Arthur spoke, the crowd fell silent, and his smile grew wider as everyone around him parted to let her and Victor through. 'We need to hurry up,' he said. 'When I asked Lord Mortimer to free you, he made me promise to bring you to him immediately. He said it was important to meet the person I was so anxious to rescue.'

At Lord Mortimer's name, Hattie sensed Victor stiffen. As they passed through the gate to enter the city, he finally spoke. 'When you meet Lord Mortimer ...' he hesitated, obviously thinking very hard. 'When you meet Lord Mortimer, just ... just be Hattie Brown. Don't mention you've met Marcia, and you mustn't let him know you've seen the Hundredth Children. It's important he doesn't realise. And remember what you said about being able to make it rain just now? Don't say that when you see him. Do you understand? He won't like it if you try to tell him you're Nimbus.'

'I'm not Nimbus. You told me that.'

The wrinkles eased in Victor's face. 'So try to avoid the subject. Be polite but give as little information as you can. Don't even tell him where you live.'

'You make it sound like something bad could happen.' Hattie felt a darkness trying to take her over, as though something bad was exactly what she expected would happen.

Victor flapped his ears. 'I'll be there to make sure it doesn't. Now look at the city. Isn't it pretty?'

He was right, it was pretty, Hattie told herself as she pushed the dark thoughts away. They had entered through one of the squares Hattie now realised were a feature of the way that the city was laid out. Behind them was the tall city wall, but the other three sides were lined with terraces of houses in soft honey-coloured stone. The most striking thing about them was the flowers. Tendrils dotted with vivid lilac blooms cascaded from the baskets that hung from every window, a waterfall of colour down the sides of the buildings.

'Where do they get the water for the flowers?' Hattie asked. 'It doesn't make sense if it doesn't rain.'

'Lord Mortimer has his ways.' Victor's voice was flat and almost drowned out by the cheers as more and more inhabitants of Somewhere-Nowhere joined the parade that was following Nimbus away from the city walls and into the heart of the city itself. Glossy-furred squirrels walked beside excited rabbits, and smiling mothers held chubby-legged toddlers high above their heads to get a better view. Laughing children leaned out from windows, throwing petals on to the crowd below. And the people and animals kept on coming until, by the time Arthur's followers reached a square that was larger and more impressive than any of the others they had passed through, they almost filled it.

'What's that?' Hattie asked, looking at a large building that dominated one side of the square. It had three extraordinary bands of windows — one star shaped, one arched, and one round.

'It's Lord Mortimer's palace.' Victor led the way to a vast door protected by two guards, each holding a long wooden staff. Lady Serena flew beside Arthur's shoulder, her head held proudly, her golden scales glowing as they caught the light.

'Aren't they coming too?' Hattie glanced back at the crowd, which had stopped just before the palace steps.

Their faces were elated. They believed, thought Hattie. They believed Arthur was Nimbus.

'They know they won't be allowed to see Lord Mortimer,' Victor told her. 'It's just us now. Are you ready?' He lowered his voice. 'Remember, no talk about being Nimbus.'

Hattie nodded. The doors opened, and she moved to join Arthur, who was waiting for her just inside the entrance of a large hall. But as soon as she got to his side, the guard moved quickly behind her, blocking the doorway.

'Victor, Gate Keeper of the Realm. You are not allowed inside.'

22

The uproar at the doors of Lord Mortimer's hall made Hattie swing round. The guards had surrounded Victor, stopping him from entering. That couldn't be! With Victor by her side she hadn't been too worried about meeting Lord Mortimer, but without him — suddenly Hattie felt as though the ground below her was moving. 'Victor, I need you,' she shouted.

'He's not going in,' one of the guards said. And, just before the doors slammed shut, she heard Victor call out. 'Remember what I told you, Hattie.'

She didn't want to have to remember. She wanted him to be by her side, protecting her. She had enough of feeling that she had to do everything for herself when she was at home.

There was a tug on her sleeve, but Hattie didn't move.

'Don't worry about Victor,' Lady Serena said. 'He's always fine in the end.' Then she laughed.

'What's funny?'

'It's just so amusing that Victor and Sir Gideon aren't

here to see Lord Mortimer with Nimbus, and I am. Isn't life wonderful sometimes?'

She circled Hattie's head. 'It's a shame we couldn't have done something about your hair and your clothes before you met him,' she said.

'What's wrong with me?'

Lady Serena sucked air through her teeth. 'Pretty much everything. Still, there's nothing we can do about it, so let's show you to Lord Mortimer as you are.'

I'm not sure I like you very much, Hattie thought as Lady Serena led her and Arthur towards where a man was sitting on a dais at the far end of the hall. Seeing them approach, he rose from the strangest seat Hattie had ever seen. The chair's wooden back was carved like a stallion rearing on its hind legs, its wild eyes glaring at whoever dared to come near. It was the most unwelcoming seat Hattie had ever seen.

As he unfurled his long body from the chair, Lord Mortimer looked as though he was stepping from a painting. His dark hair was the colour of ebony against the pale translucence of his skin. And as he tilted his head towards them, his cheeks looked as though they were carved from alabaster.

He smiled, and Hattie felt a chill run down her spine. How could he act as though he liked human-realm children when he kept so many caged behind the Keep? And how was it possible that nobody else seemed to be bothered about it? Even Victor. He might be sad, but he wasn't trying to help them. It was as though she was the only one who could see that something terrible was happening.

'Arthur, you've returned with your friend.' Lord Mortimer put out a bony hand. 'Come, human-realm child.'

He beckoned to Hattie. 'Come into the light so I can see you.'

Lady Serena nudged Hattie's shoulder. 'Go on.'

'And who are you?' Lord Mortimer asked as she got near.

'Hattie Brown.'

'Ah yes, Hattie Brown. I've been wanting to meet you. I've heard so much about you. I hear you came without a permit.' He tutted. 'That's a very unfortunate situation — you see, that's not allowed.'

He took a step closer, and Hattie tried not to react. Every part of her wanted to shout about the caged children, but Victor's words rang in her ears. Give him as little information as possible, she thought, before remembering that Victor had also told her to be polite.

'Coming to Somewhere-Nowhere without a permit's not allowed,' Lord Mortimer said again. 'Do you understand?'

This time Hattie nodded. 'I'm sorry,' she said quietly, wondering what Lord Mortimer would say if he knew about the permit in her pocket.

'Oh, don't apologise, human-realm child. It's not your fault. You didn't choose to come here yourself. I hear a foolish knight dragon and a fridge elephant brought you here.'

From somewhere near to one of the windows above them, Hattie heard a noise. She looked up. It came from close to where one of the windows was slightly open. For a moment she thought she saw a fluttering — something like a small dragon. But Lord Mortimer didn't seem to have noticed the noise. He went on. 'Which knight dragon and which fridge elephant?'

Hattie stared into the dark pupils of Lord Mortimer's eyes. She wished she knew what she was supposed to say.

'You look uncomfortable, child.' Lord Mortimer's voice was soothing. 'Don't worry, I already know who it was. I just wanted to see if you'd tell me. It's so surprising, really. Sir Gideon and Victor — I wouldn't have expected them to break the rules like that. Naughty Sir Gideon. Naughty Victor.'

'To be fair, it was Victor who took her,' Lady Serena told him. 'Sir Gideon just happened to be in the human-realm child's house when it happened.'

'Is that true, child?'

Hattie didn't say anything.

'It's true,' Lady Serena said.

'Just Victor.' Lord Mortimer's eyes narrowed. 'That's interesting, very interesting. And why do you think he did that?'

'I don't know.' Hattie's heart was thumping hard against her chest.

'Didn't he say?'

'No.'

'But he wouldn't have pulled you through for no reason.' Lord Mortimer's face shot towards Hattie, forcing her to take a step back. 'I don't believe you,' he said.

'I ...'

'Speak up. What did you do to make him bring you through?'

'I ...'

'Yes?'

'He told me not to say.'

Beside her, Lady Serena gasped.

Lord Mortimer smiled and Hattie saw the sharp points

of his teeth, like the peaks of small mountains. She swallowed hard.

'Tell me what Victor told you not to say,' Lord Mortimer insisted.

'He was embarrassed because he'd made a mistake,' Hattie started, thinking she might not like lying, but on this occasion, she'd forgive herself. 'He thought I saw him, but in fact I didn't. I only heard a squeak when I was getting something out of the fridge and accidentally hit him. But I didn't actually see him until I got here, and by then it was too late.'

Out of the corner of her eye, she could see Lady Serena studying her. *You know I'm lying*, Hattie thought. *But please don't say anything.*

Hattie looked at Lord Mortimer. His dark gaze wrapped itself around her so she couldn't tell what he was thinking. Was he like Lady Serena? Did he also know she was lying?

Suddenly Lord Mortimer snapped his fingers. 'Accidents will happen,' he said almost cheerfully. 'We'll have a word with Victor. But don't worry, nothing bad will happen to him. And we'll find a special place for you. Somewhere you can be very useful.'

'Thank you, but actually I'd like to go home, please. My mother will be getting worried about me.' Lord Mortimer didn't need to know that she'd try to help the Hundredth Children first.

Lord Mortimer shook his head.

'But I want to go home.'

'It isn't about what you want, Hattie.'

'But ... my mother isn't good on her own. She needs me.'

'No!' One of the guards slammed his staff on the flagstone floor. The sound echoed through the hall. He looked like the next time he would slam the staff into her. If only Victor was there to stop that happening.

'Don't make me tell you again,' Lord Mortimer said before swivelling to face Lady Serena and Arthur.

'There, Arthur, I did what you asked. I took the human-realm girl from the cells. See how good I've been to you.' He put one hand on Arthur's shoulder and beckoned Lady Serena towards him with the other.

'Lady Serena, I've heard how Victor misguidedly brought Hattie Brown to the Realm. Would you like to tell me how you came to bring dear Arthur here.'

'I knew he was Nimbus from the moment I arrived in his house.' Lady Serena's wings flickered with golden lights as she spoke.

'And what made you know that?'

Lady Serena modestly lowered her head. 'I found something in the house.'

'Yes.' Lord Mortimer's eyes brightened.

Lady Serena took out a neat velvet bag that was tucked under one of her wings and pulled something from it. She started to unwrap it. As the last piece of fabric fell back, Arthur called out, 'That's mine.'

'For a while perhaps,' Lord Mortimer said. 'But I'm its rightful owner.'

He reached over and picked up a small metal triangle. It was etched with something Hattie couldn't quite see.

'If this proves to be what I think it is, you have no right to it.' Lord Mortimer held the metal triangle up to the light, turning it carefully so he could see it from every angle. Then he spoke to Arthur. 'But of course, if it proves to be what I think it is, that means you are Nimbus, and I will have to act accordingly.' He bowed respectfully to Arthur before turning his attention back to the triangle.

'I've waited a long time to see this. Shall we see what it does?' He walked towards a wooden table at the side of the hall and picked up something the shape of a squat metal bottle. Engraved on its side, Hattie could see a parade of elephants, dragons, cockatoos, and many of the other creatures she'd seen in Somewhere-Nowhere. As Lord Mortimer twisted it in his hand, Hattie saw some of the pattern was missing from the bottom. Even though the blank area looked more like a star than a triangle, Lord Mortimer smiled. He placed the triangle into the hole. As soon as he let go, it tumbled on to the floor.

Lord Mortimer turned. His face was thunderous. His black eyes fixed on to Lady Serena and Arthur. 'That isn't Nimbus. Take him.'

A guard grabbed Arthur's arm, twisting it round.

'But he *is* Nimbus.' Lady Serena was quivering.

'He's no such thing.'

'But I know.'

'Don't fool around with me.'

'We have proof.'

'Take him away,' Lord Mortimer ordered the guard. 'And don't spare him.'

'No!' Lady Serena fluttered around the guard, trying to distract him.

'Take him.'

'He can make it rain,' she cried.

Lord Mortimer stared at Arthur. 'Is that true?'

'Yes.'

Lord Mortimer's bony thumbs circled each other. A slow smile crept over his face. 'Then, my dear Arthur, I must see you do it.' Lord Mortimer nodded to the guard clamped to Arthur's arm. 'Take him outside.'

23

There was a cheer from the crowd waiting in the square as the doors to the palace opened and Arthur appeared. But as soon as they saw the expression on his and Lady Serena's faces, an uneasy quiet fell upon them. A cockatoo flew from its perch on one of the window boxes. It swooped on to Hattie's shoulder and peered into her face. 'What happening? Why Lady Serena scared?' it demanded.

'Nimbus is going to show Lord Mortimer how he can make it rain.' Hattie tried to sound confident. But even as she said it, she didn't feel sure. How could Arthur make it rain properly on his own? As far as she knew, he'd never done that. And Lord Mortimer didn't seem to be the type of person who took kindly to disappointment.

'And why guard?' The cockatoo's black tongue waggled in front of her.

'He's here to make sure Nimbus doesn't get mobbed.' Hattie tried to sound cheerful.

The cockatoo nodded and flew back to the crowd, telling them that they were about to see Nimbus perform another miracle. As the news spread, the tension evaporated and the cheering began again. Hattie seemed to be the only one who didn't want to celebrate.

Everyone started to skip and dance as though they were following a carnival. They left the square and retraced the route they'd followed not long before. When families called from their windows, asking what was happening, they called back cheerfully that Lord Mortimer was going to see Nimbus make it rain for himself. The news acted like an invitation. More smiling men, women, and children joined the clapping, twirling crowd. More rabbits, squirrels, and hedgehogs danced to the gate in the city wall that was closest to the Keep. And they kept clapping and twirling down the track lined with notices displaying the sombre faces of men, women, rabbits, and pangolins below the words NOTHING IS FORGOTTEN, as if no bad thing could happen in Somewhere-Nowhere ever again.

Arthur, his guard, and Lady Serena led the way with Lord Mortimer just behind, flanked by two more guards. Nobody seemed to notice that Hattie had slipped to the back. She watched as people along their route smiled and cheered Arthur. But when they saw Lord Mortimer, even though they stayed smiling, they fell silent. No one looked him in the eye.

Eventually, they reached the Keep. Arthur's guard strode up to the door and banged on it loudly until the Cloud Keeper put his head out of the window above them. He grinned when he saw Arthur. 'Back to show off your trick, are you?' he called down. Then he caught sight of Lord Mortimer. 'S-sir,' he stuttered. 'To wh-what do I owe this honour?'

Lord Mortimer's face was unreadable as he stared up at the man. 'My dear Arthur has promised to show me how he can make it rain. When I see that, I will be the one who is honoured.' Hattie watched him incline his head towards Arthur. She was pretty certain he was playing with him.

'Please release a cloud so we may all be amazed,' Lord Mortimer ordered.

The flustered Cloud Keeper closed the window and soon the area around the Keep echoed with the clanking of his hobnailed boots on the stairs. At the top he pretended to adjust his cloak, trying not to puff in front of Lord Mortimer. Then he braced himself against something round, forcing all his bulk against it.

'Free the cloud,' a man close to Hattie called up. 'Free it now.'

The guard gave a final shove and the top of the Keep opened. A cloud sprang into the air. It bobbed up and down for a few seconds before floating towards the crowd.

Hattie forced her nails into the palms of her hands and tried to think about what Victor had told her. She mustn't do anything, either to help Arthur or to show that she knew that there were caged children on the other side of the wall behind them. She watched Arthur and Lady Serena. They seemed much calmer than they'd been when they'd left the hall. Anyone would think that there wasn't going to be a problem. And, of course, there shouldn't be. She remembered what Victor had said. She wasn't the difference as to whether or not Arthur could make it rain. So why was she feeling so nervous for him now? Hattie held her necklace, as though it might bring her luck.

'My dear Arthur, please show me what you can do.' Lord Mortimer gestured towards the cloud.

Arthur looked up at it and smiled. He walked forwards, so he was directly under it. Then he bowed, first at Lord Mortimer, then at the crowd. Finally, he looked upwards again. He opened his arms and stretched them up into the sky. 'I command you to rain,' he called out and the crowd cheered.

Above him, the cloud shivered and a few raindrops fell.

'More!' the crowd shouted.

Arthur's hands went higher. 'Rain.'

A few more drops emerged.

'More!' the crowd cried out.

Light drops pattered on their shoulders.

'More! More!'

Arthur smiled. He launched his hands to the sky. 'Rain.'

'More!' the crowd roared as a few drops gently sprinkled the ground and flowers sprang up where they had fallen.

'And again,' Arthur said.

But the cloud stopped quivering.

'I command you to rain,' Arthur boomed.

The crowd fell silent.

'Rain.'

The cloud did nothing.

Arthur's expression became uncertain. Lord Mortimer's expression darkened. Lady Serena's scales turned ghost grey, as if the life had been snatched from her.

Hattie didn't know what to do. She wanted to rush under the cloud to help, but Victor's warning filled her head. She wished he was there, to help her.

'Rain.' Arthur's voice was desperate. 'I command you to rain.'

As he uttered the final words, the cloud drifted away.

Arthur turned to look at Lord Mortimer. Lady Serena turned to look at Lord Mortimer. The crowd turned to look at Lord Mortimer. Nobody said anything.

Lord Mortimer stood very still before arching his back and pointing to the guards. 'Take the human-realm children and Lady Serena away.' His gaze swept over the crowd and he gestured towards it. 'Take some of them, too,' he told the guards. 'Teach them not to be taken in by liars. And don't be kind.'

One guard grabbed Arthur's shoulder. Another guard held Lady Serena's wing. And as Hattie saw the third turning to find her, she heard Sir Gideon's voice in her ear. 'Run as fast as you can.'

24

Hattie ran and she ran and she ran.

'Faster,' Sir Gideon urged. 'We've got to get to the Time Worm as quickly as we can.' He flew before her, his wings just a blur they were flapping so fast.

'How far is she?' Hattie panted, wondering whether it was possible to die from puffing too much.

'Far enough.' Sir Gideon took a sharp right turn.

Hattie pounded after him, choking as the red dust billowed up under her feet. He didn't seem to be making any allowance for the fact she couldn't fly, so she found herself ducking under fences and scrambling through bushes, pounding down tracks and swerving around boulders, until eventually they came to the brow of a large hollow. Below them, lay the Time Worm, curled around a large rock. Her head rested on its top, with her chin drooping over the sides, like icing dribbling from the top of a cake.

'But I didn't smell her first,' Hattie said.

'That's very rude,' Sir Gideon told her. 'The Time Worm doesn't smell unless she's drilling. Do you go around calling everyone in manual work smelly? Hello, Marcia,' he called down. 'We need you to make a hole. You need to send Hattie Brown back where she came from.'

'But I can't go yet,' Hattie said.

'You have to.'

'I won't leave Arthur.'

'We aren't safe with you here. They've already arrested Lady Serena. Just think what the guards will do to one of the dragons who led the Battle of the Three Volcanoes. They hate the fact we get more credit than them for winning, and they'd love to get even.'

You mean just think what they'd do to you if you were arrested, Hattie thought. *That isn't going to stop me helping him.* 'I won't go without my friend,' she said.

'You don't have any friends.'

Sir Gideon's words were like a slap. 'Yes, I do,' she snapped back.

'No, you don't. I heard you tell your mother.'

'But —' Hattie didn't know what to say. Sir Gideon was right. That was what she'd told her mother. But now things felt different. The whole of her life felt different.

'Is someone in trouble?' the Time Worm asked, tears swelling in her eyes.

'Yes. Arthur,' Hattie said.

'Yes. Lady Serena,' Sir Gideon said. 'Lord Mortimer had them both arrested,' Sir Gideon added.

'But why?' The Time Worm's lips were beginning to quiver.

'Lady Serena thought she'd found the Lost Seal, but she hadn't,' Sir Gideon said.

So that's what the piece of metal was about, Hattie thought.

'And then she tried to plead with him to let Arthur show him how he could make it rain.'

So if he knew that, it was Sir Gideon Hattie had seen near the broken window in Lord Mortimer's palace.

A tear fell from the Time Worm's cheek, and a daisy sprang up where it had hit the ground. 'So what happened when Nimbus tried to make it rain?' she asked.

Sir Gideon snorted. 'He isn't Nimbus. He couldn't get more than a small shower from the cloud.'

Hattie stopped herself from adding 'on his own'.

'And Lord Mortimer arrested them for that?' the Time Worm wailed. 'This is a very dark day. We must talk to Victor about it.'

Sir Gideon snorted again. 'Victor left me on my own. Yet again he's proved himself to be a coward when it comes to facing danger.'

'*You* left me on my own,' Hattie said as the Time Worm coughed. But Sir Gideon continued, puffing out his chest as he spoke.

'The reason I know what went on inside the hall, Hattie, is because I was there. You could say that I insisted on finding a way inside so I could protect you. When Victor was barred from the hall, he didn't know what to do, but I suggested flying through an open window. He begged me not to put myself in such danger, but I insisted that I must be there to know what happened to you myself.'

The Time Worm shook her head.

'Without me, Hattie Brown, you would have been abandoned.'

'Is that true?' a voice came in. 'You really can be a vexatious dragon at times, Sir Gideon. Do you go out of your way to annoy?'

'Victor.' Hattie leaned over the edge of a hollow to see

where the voice was coming from. Her heart swelled as she saw him gazing up at her, and she scrambled down the slope to reach him. 'They've arrested Arthur and Lady Serena.' She heard her voice wobble as she thought about how Arthur might be in Manchester now, not in a cell, if she'd told him about the Time Worm when he'd said he wanted to go home. 'But I didn't say anything, just like you told me,' she added, trying to push away the guilt.

'Say anything about what?' Sir Gideon asked.

'About Marcia.' Victor said. 'I told Hattie not to mention that she'd met Marcia.' He patted Hattie's shoulder with his trunk as he spoke.

'You did that for me?' The Time Worm hiccoughed through grateful sobs. 'Someone was kind to me?'

Hattie smiled to herself. Clever Victor. He'd got her out of having to make some awkward excuses. 'Victor told me how scared Marcia is of Lord Mortimer,' she agreed, thinking how often she'd lied since coming to Somewhere-Nowhere. 'He told me not to mention her.'

'That's very good, Hattie. Very good.' Victor was smiling, too. 'Now what are we going to do about Arthur and Lady Serena?'

'First we'll get rid of *her*.' Sir Gideon glanced at Hattie as he spoke. 'Then we'll go and rescue Lady Serena.'

'I'm not going without Arthur.'

'See,' Sir Gideon said, 'this is what she's been like ever since they were arrested.'

'Sir Gideon's right,' Victor said. 'You really should go back. We'll sort out Arthur.'

Hattie felt the steel harden inside her. She couldn't go home and leave them to 'sort out Arthur'. Who knew what that meant they'd do? She'd seen what they did with children here. 'No,' she said.

'There she goes again.'

'It's better that way.' Victor's voice was soothing.

'You can't send me back without letting me try to help Arthur. He came to the cell when I needed saving. And he saved you, too. I have to do the same for him.'

Victor stared deeply into her eyes, as if he was studying something.

Please don't try to stop me, Hattie begged silently.

Victor's gaze seemed to reach deep inside her. *Please, Victor, please*, she thought. *I don't know why I trust you, but I do. Please trust me, too.*

Eventually the focus of Victor's gaze changed. 'I understand,' he said gently.

'No — no you don't,' Sir Gideon yelled.

'And there's one more thing,' Hattie said. 'I have to rescue the others, too.'

'What others?' Sir Gideon shrieked. 'What's she talking about now?' Then his diamond-shaped pupils narrowed. He fluttered to the ground as he realised what she was saying. 'No! No! No!'

Victor ignored him. 'I see you have to do that, Hattie,' he told her. 'But if you stay, you'll have to be very brave. Are you prepared for what might happen?'

'Yes,' Hattie said, hoping that it was true.

25

The light was as bright as ever when Hattie, Sir Gideon, and Victor set off. 'Where are we going?' Hattie asked as Victor placed her on his back so she didn't have to walk.

'Back to the Keep. You need to see properly what you're up against.' Victor didn't break his stride. 'Don't worry, they won't expect you to go back there so soon. They'll be looking for you in other places.'

Hattie swallowed hard. Of course they would be looking for her but, up until that moment, she'd been able to push that from her mind. She put her head down and concentrated on the back of Victor's neck, telling herself that in any other circumstances riding on an elephant's back would be the most exciting thing in the world. But the image of Lord Mortimer's guards and what was happening to Arthur haunted her head. And the only thing that would replace it was the thought of her mother, alone in Worcester, wondering why Hattie wasn't there. Hattie leaned closer to Victor. 'When you were in our house, did you see my mother?' she asked.

Victor's ears twitched. 'Only when she came to the fridge,' he said.

'Did she look happy?'

'Not always.' Victor hesitated. 'But I heard her laughing with you sometimes. And I knew she was happy then.'

Nestled in the dip between Victor's shoulder blades, Hattie nodded. 'I love it when she smiles,' she told him under her breath. She waited a moment before adding, 'Sometimes everything feels too much, and I wonder whether I'm like her.'

Victor took a few more slow paces before answering. 'Even if you are, you're strong, Hattie Brown. I've only known you a short while, but I can see that.'

The skin against Hattie's cheek seemed to soften as if he understood, and Hattie thought this might be the moment to ask him something that had been troubling her. 'You know about the Hundredth Children, but you haven't tried to help them until now,' she said.

The skin under her cheek stiffened again and Victor sighed. 'I'm not proud of that, Hattie. I thought we needed the children for the good of Somewhere-Nowhere. I told myself they were here only for a while. I told myself it was okay because eventually they went back to their families and we made sure they didn't remember what they'd been through. Sometimes you get caught up in something because you tell yourself there's no other option. And when that happens it's hard to see what's right and wrong. It takes someone else to show you. That's what you've done. You've shown me what I should have done all along.'

'But you didn't always want me here. You kept trying to send me back.'

'I thought it would be safer for you. But every time I nearly sent you back, you'd do something that would make

140

me change my mind. You don't always make things easy, Hattie Brown.' He raised his trunk and wrapped it around her waist to lower her down. 'This is what we've come to see.'

He was staring into the distance, looking at the Keep, where Arthur had tried to make it rain. 'I'm sorry, I didn't tell you about the Time Worm,' Hattie whispered as if Arthur could hear her. 'I'll make it all right. I'll get you home.'

'How do we make sure the Cloud Keeper doesn't see us?' she said louder.

'There's a way.' Victor went over to a tree. He put his trunk on one of the lower branches and counted the twigs. 'That one.' As he pressed, the tree bowed and shifted to reveal a hole. Below it, a short drop from where they stood, was a sparkling stream.

'What's that?'

'It goes from behind the tower to the centre of the city. It's our way to the Keep. Jump down.'

Hattie dangled her legs over the opening. 'It isn't poisoned, is it?' she asked, remembering the Knowledge Worm's spit.

Victor smiled. 'No, this is fine.'

As Hattie lowered herself down, Sir Gideon flew past her through the gap. He didn't say anything. He hadn't said anything since Victor had agreed to let her help rescue Arthur. And if it was possible for a knight dragon to fly grumpily, that's what Sir Gideon had done.

He opened a wooden box that sat on a ledge, close to where they'd entered. From inside, he took a lantern and a long match. 'Couldn't you have done that with your breath?' Hattie said, as he struck the match.

Sir Gideon glared at her. 'That would be against the

Knight Dragons' Code. And we're in enough trouble already.' He turned his back as something blocked the light that was coming in from outside. Victor was trying to force himself through the hole.

'Mind yourselves. I'm coming down.' There was a noise a bit like a cork popping, and Victor landed on his bottom in the water. 'That was a squeeze.' He stood up and shook silvery drops from his hide. Then he looked in both directions down the tunnel. 'This way.' He started off.

'So if this isn't spittle, and if there's a drought in Somewhere-Nowhere, what's this water?'

'You'll see.'

They started down the stream. The flickering shadows of an elephant, a dragon, and a girl matched them step for step, breath for breath, until Victor finally stopped. 'Here.' He pushed against a large round disc in the tunnel roof, allowing Sir Gideon to flutter out.

'Get on my back, Hattie.' Victor bent his knee to make a step for her.

'But what about you?' Hattie asked as she heaved herself up. How was a portly elephant supposed to get out of a tunnel like this?

'I have a less dignified way of getting there. Stay with Sir Gideon until I arrive.'

'What did you do to the ledger the guard had at the Anywhere Office?' Hattie said to Sir Gideon as Victor set off down the tunnel.

'I forged it.'

'You nearly got away with it,' Hattie said, trying to sound extra friendly.

'If you weren't here, I wouldn't need to do things like that.' Sir Gideon turned away until they heard Victor's voice coming through the darkness.

'Well, you two seem to be getting on famously,' he said. As he came closer, Hattie saw that his hide was studded with thorns.

'You're hurt.'

'Not really. It's more irritating than anything. They take ages to get off.'

Hattie picked a few of the spikey studs from his ears. 'Feel free to help,' she said to Sir Gideon.

'I will when someone helps me by getting rid of you.'

'Ignore him,' Victor said. 'The important thing is what's over there.' He turned slowly, and Hattie saw that they were close to the cage where the Hundredth Children were kept. A shiver chased down her spine. Behind the bars were hundreds of pairs of eyes. They were big, they were haunted, they were staring. And they were staring at her.

'How can there be so many of them and so little sound?'

The wrinkles on Victor's face tightened. 'There's a special pollen that's scattered on the ground within the compound. Over time, it subdues them and the longer they've been there, the quieter they become. Only leaving the compound breaks the pollen's power. By the look of them, most of these children have been here a while.' He turned back to Hattie. 'Shall we go to them?'

Hattie didn't move. Her feet felt like concrete. She stared back at the hollow-cheeked faces.

'You need to go to them, Hattie.'

Hattie dug her nails deep into the palms of her hand. She wished her mother was here. She wanted to hold on to someone, but it couldn't be Victor or Sir Gideon.

'Hattie.'

'Of course we should go to them.' She tried to sound confident, even though her insides were like jelly.

She forced her feet forwards, and as she got closer, she

realised the children weren't completely silent after all. Her footsteps were marked by shallow breaths, like dogs panting after a chase. The sound of them made her want to turn and run, but she pushed herself to take one step, then another, then another, until she could properly see the faces from which the strange panting came. Every one of the children inside the cage was about her age.

'Why are they here?'

'They've been brought here. Some time ago, a dragon accidentally brought a human-realm child back to Some-where-Nowhere, thinking he was Nimbus. He wasn't, but now every hundredth quest the knight dragons go on to your human realm, they bring back a child. Usually, they're about eleven. We've tried younger and we've tried a bit older. But your age seems to work the best.'

'Work the best for what?'

'For making it rain.'

'But ...' She stopped. None of this made sense.

She leaned over and touched one of the bars, trying to understand what Victor was saying. A hand grabbed at her fingers. Hattie snatched them away.

'You know I told you every human-realm child could make a cloud give up a few drops of rain? We found that out when the human-realm child was brought here by accident. And if you get lots of children under a cloud you can get it to rain properly. We used to throw stones at the clouds and hope they'd give us a few drops. But then we realised what human-realm children could do for us. So Lord Mortimer gets the Time Worm to steal the clouds and the knight dragons bring the Hundredth Children here. When the city needs more rain, they bring the clouds over and capture the water the children produce. And it's sent to the rest of the city through the underground streams.'

Hattie stared into the eyes of the girl who'd tried to grab her hand and another shock ran through her body. It was the red-headed girl she'd seen trussed in a guard's cloak when she'd first arrived in Somewhere-Nowhere. She tried a half-smile, to see if the girl recognised her, but her eyes were empty. It was as if all the life had been drawn out of her.

'Is this where Arthur is?' she said.

Victor flicked his ears. 'I suspect so.'

And this was where they would have put her. Hattie would have been as lifeless as the girl standing in front of her. 'What's your name?' she asked.

The girl stared back at her but didn't respond.

'I'm Hattie.'

'Beth.' It was barely a rasp.

'Beth, I'm looking for someone. Have you seen a boy called Arthur? He'll be new.'

Beth stared at her blankly.

'Please, Beth.'

After a few moments, the girl nodded. 'Yes,' she whispered. 'He's here.'

'Can I see him?'

The girl shook her head and pointed slowly to the other side of the compound.

'Don't do it, Hattie,' Victor said.

'Do what?'

'Don't call for him.'

'How did you know I was about to do that?'

Victor shrugged. 'It would be the natural thing to do. But they mustn't know we're here. Not yet. I just wanted you to see the compound properly, not just what you saw before. You need to know what you'd be taking on if you really want to rescue them. It won't be easy.' He started to move. 'We need to go to the Guild to mobilise the dragons.'

'We can't just go.' Hattie stayed where she was.

'We have to. We can't stay here. Lord Mortimer doesn't want anyone interfering with the children. If the Cloud Keeper spots us, he'll call the guards.' Victor's trunk touched her shoulder.

'But ...' Hattie started again. Then she stopped. She couldn't do this on her own. She had to trust Victor. Without saying anything more, she turned to follow him. They'd nearly reached the entrance to the underground stream before she spoke. 'I have to do it. I have to rescue all of them.'

Beside them, there was a cry. Sir Gideon's wings beat even more furiously. 'How did this happen to me?' he wailed.

26

S ir Gideon didn't stop complaining during the whole of
their journey back to the city. But by the time they
reached the Guild of the Knight Dragons' building, his
anger was beginning to subside.

'I suppose you want me to get us in,' he said, but he
didn't wait for a reply before flying to a small recess in the
wall. Almost as soon as he'd settled, his scales began to
change from green, to blue, to grey. The edges of his wings
started to blend with the brickwork behind him, so that soon
Hattie couldn't make them out at all. His legs and body
disappeared. And then, when the only things that were
visible were his blinking eyes, part of the wall in front of
them opened up.

'Did ... did Sir Gideon just do that?' Hattie asked
Victor.

'That's how the knight dragons make sure no one
outside the Guild can get in,' Victor replied as though there
was nothing remarkable about a wall moving by itself.

The colour at the edges of Sir Gideon's wings was

turning green again. 'Run in quickly, before it closes up,' he said.

They dashed forward and Hattie found herself racing into a large hallway. 'We're going to watch from up here,' Victor told her. He started up some shallow stone steps just wide enough to take an elephant, giving Hattie no time to see the wall close behind them. Following him, she found herself on a broad balcony overlooking an area that was alive with light. It bounced off the hundreds of silver crests that crammed the walls.

'Where are we?' she asked, twisting to see behind a pillar. The crests really were everywhere.

'It's the Guild's great chamber, where the dragons come together to debate.'

Now that Hattie's eyes were adjusting to the brightness, she could see that the crests were decorated with coats of arms, and above each crest was a tangled twist of metal. 'And what are those?' she asked, pointing to the one that was nearest.

'When the knight dragons swear their oath to the Guild, they breathe fire one last time to melt a sword. After that, breathing fire is forbidden unless they do it in defence of the Realm. Those swords are here to remind them of their vows.' Victor glanced over at Sir Gideon. 'Are we in time?'

'I think they'll still be debating,' he said.

Victor led them to a low rail at the edge of the balcony. From there, Hattie could peer down into the large circular chamber. Below her, was a swirl of colour. Rows of tiny benches surrounded a podium that dominated the centre of the room. On them, golden-, cerise-, emerald-, silver-, and magenta-coloured dragons stood side by side. One dragon was apart on the podium. He was larger than either Lady

Serena or Sir Gideon and wore a breastplate on which a dragon rose from the crater of a volcano.

'Sir Willow-Wood,' Sir Gideon whispered. 'If he's speaking, this is very serious.'

Hattie leaned further over the rail to hear what was being said, but Sir Gideon tugged at her hair. 'Not too far. You shouldn't be obvious. They won't mind Victor being here but it's best if they don't see you until the vote is over.'

'Fellow knight dragons,' Sir Willow-Wood was saying. 'We are gathered here on a very dark day for our Guild.'

'Indeed,' Sir Gideon muttered.

'One of our members has been arrested and flung into the Keep with the Hundredth Children. This is the first time a dragon has been jailed in the history of the Guild.'

There was a murmuring around the benches.

'Since its beginnings, the Guild has existed with the purpose to defend the Realm. We vow to hold this purpose above all other things and to sacrifice ourselves to that purpose if we are called upon to do so. We've been honoured for our work as a Guild and as individuals.' Sir Willow-Wood bowed. 'I myself have been honoured for leading the Battle of the Three Volcanoes against The Traitor.'

'Not on your own,' Sir Gideon muttered.

'Since he came to rule over us as Lord Protector of Somewhere-Nowhere, we've been at Lord Mortimer's side, making sure the Realm and its inhabitants are safe.'

'Yes.' Sir Gideon joined in the general agreement in the chamber.

'But something has happened to change all of that. Lady Serena has brought shame upon us all.'

This time Sir Gideon shook his head.

'She's brought dishonour on us in Lord Mortimer's eyes. She brought back a child from the human realm who isn't one of the Hundredth Children.'

Beside Hattie, both Victor and Sir Gideon shifted position uneasily.

'She claimed that he was Nimbus.' Sir Willow-Wood stamped his foot. 'She claimed she'd found the Lost Seal.' He stamped his foot again.

'But no! She hadn't found the Lost Seal. And Arthur Handley-Bennett wasn't Nimbus. Lady Serena has betrayed the Realm of Somewhere-Nowhere with her false-hoods. She's betrayed Lord Mortimer. She's betrayed the Guild.'

A murmur of agreement went around the chamber. The colour of the knight dragons had changed. Now almost every one of them was vermillion red. And Sir Willow-Wood was reddest of them all. 'I tell you, brothers and sisters of the Guild of Knight Dragons, Lady Serena must be cast out. She isn't worthy to be among our number. We must banish her from our midst.'

'Yes!' The other knight dragons started to stamp their feet as the noise in the chamber swelled. 'Banish her. Banish her,' came the cry. 'Banish her now.'

Sir Willow-Wood raised his wings. 'Do we agree to vote on whether to banish Lady Serena?'

'Yes,' the dragons chorused.

'No!' Sir Gideon yelled.

Every face in the chamber turned up to the balcony and Hattie shrank even further back, hoping she hadn't been spotted.

'Sir Gideon,' Sir Willow-Wood snarled. 'Do you wish to speak against Lady Serena? She is condemned already.

Even you may find it difficult to say anything worse about her.'

'I want to speak, but not to condemn her.'

Sir Willow-Wood looked puzzled. 'I thought you weren't Lady Serena's friend anymore.'

'I'm not, but I can't let you cast her out without anyone speaking for her.'

'We asked for someone to do that at the beginning, but no one came forward.'

'I come forward now.'

Sir Willow-Wood sighed. 'We need to get on. We are all busy dragons.'

'It's Lady Serena's right to have a champion when she's not here.'

Sir Willow-Wood moved from the podium. 'Very well. Every member of the Guild has that right, even when they don't deserve it.'

Sir Gideon flew to where Sir Willow-Wood had been standing. He turned slowly until he had the attention of every dragon in the chamber.

'My brother and sister dragons,' he began. 'Lady Serena has done a shameful thing. She's brought a child from the human-realm to Somewhere-Nowhere who isn't Nimbus or one of the Hundredth Children.' For a second his gaze locked with Victor's before moving on. 'By doing that, Lady Serena has gone against the Code of the Knight Dragons.'

Sir Willow-Wood smiled at him and the dragons in the chamber brayed and stamped their feet.

Sir Gideon waited for the noise to die down. 'We know that the punishment for breaking the Code is banishment from the Guild.'

The cheer went up again.

'And yet I don't believe that Lady Serena should be banished.'

Sir Willow-Wood frowned and the chamber fell silent.

'Each of us has gone on many quests. We know what we are asked to do. We swear the oath each time we leave. We know we must only bring back one of the Hundredth Children or a child with the Lost Seal. We swear this every time we go into the human realm.

'Arthur Handley-Bennett wasn't one of the Hundredth Children, Lady Serena knew that. But she did think that she'd found the Lost Seal and therefore that Arthur Handley-Bennett was Nimbus. She did exactly what she'd sworn to do. She did exactly what each of us swears to do every time we go on a quest. The object she brought back wasn't the Lost Seal. Arthur Handley-Bennett isn't Nimbus. But Lady Serena did what she was supposed to do. She did her duty.'

A low murmur went around the chamber.

'But ...' Sir Willow-Wood began.

'You have spoken, Sir Willow-Wood,' Sir Gideon said. 'It's my turn now.'

'Any one of us could be imprisoned in the Keep now instead of Lady Serena. Any one of us could be imprisoned for keeping our vows. She hasn't dishonoured the Guild, she has honoured it. And she's paid a high price. Now we should keep the vow we made to each other when we joined the Guild. We promised to be brothers and sisters. We said we'd support and defend each other as well as the Realm. Lord Mortimer knows this, just as every other ruler of Somewhere-Nowhere has known it. That bond we have to each other has always been respected, whoever's in power. Lady Serena is in the Keep, but it could have been you.' Sir Gideon pointed to one of the dragons. 'It could have been you.' He pointed to another. 'Or you. Or you. It could have been any one of us who had carried out a quest as we had sworn to do.'

The scales of the dragons changed to fiery orange.

'I urge you to vote, but not to banish her. I urge you to save her. I urge you to save the honour of the Guild. I urge you to vote to save a member who was just keeping her vows.'

'We can't have two votes — and we've already agreed to vote on whether to banish her,' Sir Willow-Wood sounded angry.

'Why can't we have two votes?'

'Because it's never been done before.'

'Has a knight dragon ever been imprisoned before?'

'Two votes — one on whether she should be banished, the other on whether she should be saved,' a dragon called out, and Hattie recognised Lady Violet's voice. She leaned a bit further and saw the dragon she'd met on her way to the city, whose kind face had made Hattie want to tell her everything about home. Lady Violet's iridescent scales flickered with the most vivid purple Hattie had ever seen. Around her, the other dragons rose from the benches and hovered anxiously in the air.

'But,' Sir Willow-Wood said.

'Two votes.' Lady Violet spoke with certainty, as if she didn't expect to be challenged again.

Sir Willow-Wood scanned the chamber. 'Very well,' he said. 'I propose that we banish Lady Serena for bringing the Guild of the Knight Dragons into disrepute. All those in favour say "aye".'

There was silence.

'And I propose that we save Lady Serena and Arthur Handley-Bennett for the honour of the Guild of the

Knight Dragons,' Sir Gideon said. 'All those in favour say "aye".'

The chamber erupted with the sound of dragons shouting.

'Very occasionally, I feel proud of that stubborn dragon,' Victor whispered to Hattie.

27

As the cheering died down, six of the dragons flew to the back of the chamber and settled in a recess. They stretched out so that each touched the other and the edges of their wings began to change to the deep mahogany stain of the wood behind them. Soon their wings were impossible to make out. Then their legs disappeared, then their bodies, until Hattie could only see six pairs of blinking eyes. The dragons snapped shut their eyelids so they vanished too. And with that, two doors below them swung open and a beam of silver light, so intense Hattie thought it might blind her, filled the chamber.

Every dragon turned to the doors, their bodies shimmering as the light danced on their scales like sun on an ocean. Their expressions were noble, purposeful, determined. Their eyes glowed like gemstones.

'Where's the light coming from?' Hattie asked, shielding her eyes.

'It's the armoury. The dragons use steel forged in a fire started with their own breath to make their armour. It's forged before they make the vow not to breathe fire, and it makes dragon-steel, which is one of the strongest metals in the Realm. But if something happens to their armour or they lose it, they can't forge more unless they leave the Guild. Otherwise, they would be breaking the code of the knight dragons.'

The dragons were lining up. One by one, each went into the armoury and came out wearing a breastplate and helmet with a sword slung across his or her body. Instead of being weighed down by them, they flew powerfully back to the benches with firm, slow beats of their wings, stronger than before.

Sir Gideon had left the podium and come to the balcony where Hattie and Victor were watching.

'You spoke well,' Victor told him. 'It took me back to the days when we all looked out for each other — before the Battle of the Three Volcanoes changed things.'

Sir Gideon nodded. 'But Sir Willow-Wood isn't happy. He's used to getting his own way.'

'There are a lot of inhabitants of our realm who have got far too used to getting their own way. But let's not concern ourselves with that now. We have Lady Serena and Arthur to worry about.' Victor smiled. 'To think, you stood up for Lady Serena. Now that really is like old times.'

Sir Gideon grimaced. 'I did it for the Guild not for Lady Serena.'

'Why wouldn't you do it for Lady Serena?' Hattie asked.

'We fell out.' Sir Gideon glanced away. 'Things like that happen,' he added.

Victor looked seriously at Sir Gideon. 'Do you have a plan?'

'We fly to the Keep. If we're lucky, they won't be expecting the whole of the Guild to attack. They wouldn't imagine that Sir Willow-Wood would let the dragons defy Lord Mortimer's wishes. They won't think we'd try to rescue Lady Serena.'

'If we're lucky.' Victor looked thoughtful. 'And assuming Sir Willow-Wood doesn't tell them.'

'He'd never do that.'

'Possibly. But Sir Willow-Wood doesn't like to be wrong,' Victor said, the creases in his forehead growing deeper. 'I've got something I need to do,' he said as Sir Gideon spread out his wings. 'It means I may not be here once you've changed into your armour. But don't forget Hattie Brown. Look after her. And remember to come back for her.'

'Where are you going?' Sir Gideon's eyes flashed with irritation.

'To buy you some time. But if I'm not back, don't wait for me. Promise me that — it's important.'

Sir Gideon snorted.

'Promise me as a member of the Guild of the Knight Dragons.'

'You don't need to go that far.'

'As a member of the Guild of the Knight Dragons.'

'Suit yourself — I promise.' Sir Gideon set off towards the armoury.

'Remember, don't forget Hattie Brown.' Victor called after him.

'As if I could.'

An uneasy feeling began to come over Hattie. 'Where are you going?'

'It's better you don't know. I'll come back, but until I do, make sure Sir Gideon keeps his promise. Stay with him. Despite everything, he's not as bad as he appears.' Victor's trunk touched her shoulder. 'Be careful, Hattie Brown.'

'Why are you speaking like that? It's like you don't really think you're going to see us later,' Hattie said, feeling a knot tighten in her stomach. She wanted to grab him and make him stay.

But Victor had already started down the shallow stone stairs to the entrance below. He was so intent on leaving that he didn't notice her following him. He didn't glance back before his trunk reached up to a lever so that the wall opened up. And he didn't see Hattie as she slipped through the gap just before it closed again, following him outside.

 28

Outside the Guild of the Knight Dragons, Hattie slid into the shadows of a doorway as she watched Victor. He'd walked thirty paces before a guard pointed the tip of a staff between his eyes.

'Halt.' The guard held the staff steady.

'How can I help you?' Victor asked.

'Have you been inside the Guild of the Knight Dragons?'

'I have.'

'Were you witness to what they were saying?'

'I was.'

'In the name of Lord Mortimer, I demand that you tell me what was said.'

'In the name of Lord Mortimer, I will tell you every word.'

Hattie held her breath as the guard smirked.

'I've heard that you've been deceived,' Victor began. 'Lady Serena did find the Lost Seal in Arthur Handley-Bennett's house, but she didn't give it to Lord Mortimer.

She kept it for herself. She tried to cheat him with a fake and hid the real Lost Seal by the caves.'

The guard smirked even more. 'Victor, first of the gate keepers, you've done well,' he said.

'The knight dragons will debate for many hours how to punish Lady Serena before they go looking for the Lost Seal themselves,' Victor continued. 'But I've heard enough to show you where it's buried so that you can take it to Lord Mortimer. You can prove to him that you're more trust-worthy than the knight dragons. You can show him that you deserve his gratitude more than them.'

'You'll take us there?' The guard's eyes flashed with excitement.

'Yes, but the area we need to cover is big. We'll need every guard you have based in the city to unearth it.'

'We'll call every man.' The guard turned to a cockatoo. 'Credo, tell them all to go to the caves.'

The cockatoo's gaze met Victor's, and he raised his crest. 'Spread word,' he said.

'Hattie, what are you doing out here?' There was a whirring of wings as Lady Violet flew in front of Hattie's face.

29

'Come inside, and get out of sight,' Lady Violet urged, flattening herself against the wall of the Guild building. 'What are you doing here?' she asked again. The tips of her wings changed from amber to a mottled pattern of greys and browns. Soon their edges became invisible against the brickwork of the wall.

'Sir Gideon took me and Victor inside to watch the debate.'

'So you were inside just now?' For a moment, the whole of Lady Violet's body was visible again as surprise flashed through her features.

'Yes.'

'Where?'

'Upstairs with Victor.'

'Then we'd better get you back there in case the guards return.'

'But what about Victor?' Hattie asked. 'What was he doing?' She wondered how much of the exchange between Victor and the guards Lady Violet had seen.

'I don't know, but, knowing him, he'll have a plan.' A

look of deep concentration came over Lady Violet's face and the tips of her wings began to merge with the walls again. First, the whole of her wings disappeared. Then her body disappeared. Then finally it was impossible to make out the contours of her face. When all Hattie could see was two blinking eyes, the wall opened up, and Lady Violet's outline broke free from the brickwork. 'Follow me,' she said, and she led Hattie into the Guild building and to the balcony where she and Victor had been not long before.

'Stay out of sight,' Lady Violet whispered before flying to the centre of the chamber.

Hattie watched as the dragons continued to fly to and from the armoury. Sir Gideon was the last to come out. The others drew back to let him pass as he emerged in his dragon-steel breastplate and helmet. He flew across the wooden benches that filled the chamber and settled on the podium before stretching out his wings to show their full span. As he moved, the crest of the Guild — a dragon rising from the crater of a volcano — became visible on his breast-plate. The light from the armour of the dragons in front of him created a shimmering halo above where they had gathered.

'Brother and sister dragons, we fly to the Keep to save our sister Lady Serena.' Sir Gideon's voice sounded deeper than usual.

Around him, the dragons stretched out their wings so that neighbour touched neighbour. Their colour changed to silver. 'We fly to the Keep,' they intoned. 'We fly to save our sister.'

'But before we do, who's this?' A menacing voice boomed from somewhere near Hattie. Sir Willow-Wood shot up from under the rail and hovered so close that Hattie could feel his breath on her face.

Every dragon in the chamber swung round to see what was happening. Anxiety cracked the room.

Hattie looked at Sir Gideon to see what she should do, but he didn't look worried. 'That is Hattie Brown,' he said as if it was the most natural thing in the world for her to be there.

'Who is Hattie Brown?'

'A human-realm child.'

'I can see that.' Sir Willow-Wood darted around Hattie's head and came back in front of her nose.

'Human-realm children can't come to the Guild.'

'Not unless they're invited. And I invited her,' Sir Gideon told him.

'Is she one of the Hundredth Children? Where are her papers?' Sir Willow-Wood tried to fly inside her pocket among the sweet wrappers, hair grips, magnifying glass, and dog whistle that were already there.

'The Knowledge Worm has them,' Sir Gideon said.

How could he stay so calm? Hattie wondered. Wasn't his heart beating as fast as hers?

'Does she?' Sir Willow-Wood sounded doubtful. He sprang back up to her face. 'Does she?' he demanded.

'I ... I came through the Anywhere Office.'

The beat of Sir Willow-Wood's wings slowed, and he pulled away from her face. 'That suggests the Knowledge Worm must have approved you.' He scowled. 'But how do you know Sir Gideon?'

'He was in my —'

'Victor introduced us.' Sir Gideon came in quickly.

'You know Victor?'

'Yes.'

The tension among the dragons in the chamber eased. One of them landed on the rail, and Hattie saw the kind face of Lady Violet again. She smiled at her. 'I've met Hattie Brown before,' she announced. 'I met her on the road, travelling with Lady Serena and Arthur Handley-Bennett. But Victor wasn't there,' she continued as though they hadn't both just watched Victor lying to the guards. 'How do you know him?'

'He brought me from Worcester.'

'Worcester?'

'My home in the human realm.' A tightness stretched across Hattie's chest when she thought about it. She'd been so focused on Arthur and the caged children, she hadn't thought about what was happening at home since she'd come back from the Keep. But her mother would be sick with worry.

'Brothers and sisters, we must fly to the Keep to rescue Lady Serena.' Sir Gideon stretched out his wings again.

'But what do we do with Hattie Brown?' another dragon asked.

Hattie tried to push the thoughts of her mother away. There was nothing she could do to help her while she was here. She had to get on with rescuing Arthur and the children. After that, she could get home to Worcester and put the broken pieces of her mother back together again. 'Take me with you,' she said.

The dragon shook his head. 'We can't do that.'

'Victor said you had to.'

'But —' Sir Willow-Wood started.

'It's true,' said Sir Gideon. 'Victor said she was to come with us to the Keep.'

'That would be irregular.' Sir Willow-Wood's eyes were icy as he spoke.

Seeing them, Hattie felt the determination growing inside her. 'Yes, that's what Victor wanted.' She looked Sir

Willow-Wood defiantly in the eye. If he tried to stop her going with the dragons, she was going to kick up a fuss. She opened her mouth to say so when Lady Violet pressed her body close to Hattie's lips. 'Let me fix your hair, it's got all messed up,' she said.

She's stopping me from saying anything more, thought Hattie.

'It would be irregular, but I'll allow it out of respect for Victor,' Sir Willow-Wood said as Hattie heard Sir Gideon's voice from the chamber below.

'Brothers and sisters, we fly to the Keep.'

'But how will I get there?' Hattie whispered as Lady Violet stopped fussing and pulled back to check her work.

'You'll see,' Lady Violet said, and tugged a last strand of hair.

30

The wall of the Guild of Knight Dragons parted, and Hattie felt herself lifted off the ground. Two dragons held her shoulders. Three dragons held each of her legs. And there were two more, one either side of her body. Together, these tiny dragons made her feel impossibly light. She glided towards the door as if carried on a current of air and flew out into the city.

Immediately, the dragons that were carrying her soared so she was looking down on the city's bustling alleyways and streets. Below her, its inhabitants had gathered for a market. They crowded around stalls selling toffee apples, lollipops, and frothing pink and purple juices; but the stalls that had once been crammed with souvenirs of Arthur's arrival were empty. Just beyond the market were three tall stone buildings, their outsides festooned with hanging baskets heavy with geraniums, begonias, and fuchsias. And further still, she looked out to the parched red dust outside the city walls. Around her was an army of dragons, over a thousand strong. It soared high above the city, out of sight of anyone, unless they happened to look up. And no one did.

So the great army of dragons flew unnoticed, silent except for the hiss of air as they moved gracefully through it.

I must remember this for ever, Hattie thought. *I must remember what it feels like to swim through the air and to float over people's heads. I must remember what it feels like not to have the ground tugging on my feet. I must remember this freedom.*

Sir Gideon flew in front of her. Like every other dragon, his body was silver-blue beneath his breastplate. If anyone had cared to look up, they would have been more likely to see a blur of light streaking through the sky than a phalanx of dragons. And whether they might see a human-realm child in the middle of the dazzling effect, Hattie couldn't tell.

Eventually they neared the Keep and the dragons slowed. For the first time since they had left the Guild, Hattie saw Sir Willow-Wood. He led the throng, his expression dark and unreadable. And when he stopped, the dragon army stopped behind him, suspended in mid-air by fluttering wings. Only Sir Gideon carried on. He went to Sir Willow-Wood's side and they spoke as the dragon army waited.

Sir Willow-Wood turned to address the army. 'Sir Gideon is going to take a small force to discover where Lady Serena is being held.' He pointed to three dragons in the front of the swarm and a hum of approval went through the army. Only Hattie seemed to be unhappy.

'I want to go, too,' she blurted out.

Sir Willow-Wood looked at her sharply.

'How typical of a human-realm child to think only of herself. This isn't about you, Hattie Brown. This is about Lady Serena. And when she's found, her brother and sister dragons will rescue her.'

And Arthur and the Hundredth Children, Hattie thought. But she didn't say anything to Sir Willow-Wood.

'Hattie Brown, the fact we have to bring you along with us is regrettable, but we cannot let it get in the way of our true aim,' Sir Willow-Wood continued.

Hattie held her tongue. If she upset the dragons who were holding her, she was in for a very nasty fall.

'The dragons will look after you until I come back,' Sir Gideon called to her, and then he and the three dragons set off, flying towards where Hattie had seen the Hundredth Children. Their bodies became smaller and smaller, until they were impossible to make out against the cloudless blue sky.

'Don't worry,' said Lady Violet, who was holding one of her shoulders. 'No one is as good at this type of thing as Sir Gideon. He'll find Lady Serena. We'll have her out in no time.' She smiled. 'And would you prefer to sit, Hattie Brown? It must feel very odd hovering on your stomach like that.'

The dragons moved so that Hattie was suspended as though she was on a chair.

'I feel like I'm a queen on a throne.'

Lady Violet smiled again.

'And what about the Hundredth Children,' Hattie asked after a while. 'How will we get them out?'

Hattie whooshed down before the dragons steadied themselves.

'Sorry about that,' one of them said. 'For a moment, we thought you were serious.'

'But I was.'

She plunged again, only this time not as far.

'Oh no,' one of the dragons said, laughing. 'We can't let them out. We're only here to help Lady Serena.'

'But Arthur is in there, too.'

'We promised to free him,' one of the other dragons reminded the dragon who was laughing.

'Dragons always keep their promises,' another said.

The first dragon stopped laughing. 'Okay, we'll free Arthur Handley-Bennett,' he agreed.

'And the Hundredth Children, too.' As she said it, Hattie braced herself in case the dragons sent her falling again.

Lady Violet cocked her head, and Hattie thought she saw a smile pass quickly over her face.

'Victor wanted us to free all the Hundredth Children,' Hattie went on.

'Victor wanted that? You're sure?' the dragon holding her left leg asked.

'Yes.'

'Victor is a remarkable elephant. He's much revered in Somewhere-Nowhere,' another of the dragons said. 'But he couldn't have wanted the Hundredth Children set free.'

'Why?'

'Where will the water come from?'

'From ...' Hattie started, then she stopped. She had no idea where the water would come from if there were no Hundredth Children to make it rain.

'Even Victor can get things wrong sometimes,' the dragon said before his attention went to the direction of the Keep. 'Look, they're coming back.'

Every dragon focused on four approaching dots. 'Have you found her?' Sir Willow-Wood called out when they were almost back with them.

'We have.' Sir Gideon looked grave. 'She's in a small cell on her own behind the compound.'

'How many dragons do we need to get inside?' Sir Willow-Wood asked.

'We won't be able to get inside.'

'Of course we will.'

'The cell is reinforced.'

'That won't stop us. We'll take the whole army if we need to.'

'It's lava iron.'

Sir Willow-Wood turned spectre grey. 'There's nothing we can do,' he said. 'Return to the Guild.'

Sir Gideon flew towards Hattie. His eyes were blank, as though something had left him.

'What's happening?' Hattie asked. She didn't like seeing him look so broken.

'Lady Serena is being held in lava iron,' he said. 'Even dragon-steel can't get through that.'

'So that's it? We're not going to rescue Lady Serena and Arthur?'

'There's nothing we can do.'

Some of the dragons had already started to leave. 'There must be something you can do,' Hattie said. She couldn't believe they were going to give up that easily.

'Lava iron comes from the Three Volcanoes. There's nothing we can do to weaken it.'

'But Victor said ...'

'Even Victor will understand when we tell him. He knows nothing can touch it.'

For the first time since she'd seen him speak on Lady Serena's behalf at the Guild of Knight Dragons, Sir Gideon looked defeated. His scales had dimmed to a dull grey, and his head drooped as though his helmet was suddenly heavy. His wings moved slowly as he prepared to follow the dragons who were going back to the city.

This couldn't be the end, Hattie thought. There must be something they could do. She couldn't be this close to rescuing Arthur and the Hundredth Children, only to fail now. She tried to think. There must be something in Somewhere-Nowhere that could get through lava iron. It couldn't be impossible.

'What if you breathed fire on it?' she asked. 'Would it melt?'

Shock flashed over Sir Gideon's face. 'We couldn't do that. All the members of the Guild have taken an oath never to breathe fire again unless it's in defence of the Realm.'

'But ...'

'It probably wouldn't work,' Sir Gideon snapped. 'And we'd be thrown out of the Guild. And that's the worst thing that can happen to a dragon. There's nothing we can do. We may as well give up.' His shoulders slumped.

No, Hattie thought. *I'm not going to give up that easily. I don't care if all the dragons have given up. I won't abandon Arthur and Lady Serena like that.*

'What about the Knowledge Worm's spittle?' she asked.

Sir Gideon stared at Hattie. His scales flashed gold.

'Come back,' he yelled at the disappearing dragon army.

31

'Hattie Brown has something to say,' Sir Gideon announced as the dragons crowded round them. 'She's got a suggestion for how we could get through the lava iron.'

Hattie swallowed hard. More than one thousand dragons were staring at her as she hovered in mid-air. One thousand dragons who didn't like human-realm children very much. And Arthur and the Hundredth Children's rescue depended on those thousand dragons thinking her idea was a good one. 'I wondered about the Knowledge Worm's spittle,' she said, suddenly thinking it didn't sound likely.

A murmur went through the nearest dragons.

'What did she say?' a dragon shouted from the back of the army.

'She's suggesting the Knowledge Worm's spittle.'

'It could work.'

'Yes.'

Sir Willow-Wood flew to where Sir Gideon was hovering. 'Why did you halt the army? I told them to return to the Guild.'

'Hattie Brown has made a suggestion I think could work.'

'What suggestion could a human-realm child make that we haven't thought of?'

'I wondered whether the Knowledge Worm's spittle could work.'

Sir Willow-Wood looked Hattie up and down as if he couldn't believe the suggestion could have been from her.

'It's our only chance of helping Lady Serena,' Lady Violet said.

'That's true,' Sir Gideon said. 'We've never tried it.'

'Maybe it could work,' Sir Willow-Wood sneered. 'But how would you get it here? There isn't a vessel in the whole of Somewhere-Nowhere it wouldn't burn through in seconds. Your plan might be good hypothetically, Hattie Brown. But that's all it is — a good idea that can't work in the real world.'

Hattie wasn't going to let him dismiss her just like that. 'But if it's so dangerous, why doesn't it destroy the banks of the streams from the Anywhere Office?' she asked.

'That's because, when they were built, they were blessed by the person who meant the most to the inhabitants of Somewhere-Nowhere. That gives it the power to withstand the poison. The inhabitants of Somewhere-Nowhere came together and chose Lord Mortimer's mother, the most honourable person who has ever lived in the Realm. Her goodness has protected the banks and the Anywhere Office ever since.'

Lady Violet's wings fluttered. 'So it might be possible,' she said. 'What if we put the spittle into something that belongs to someone good? Someone who has integrity.'

The frown lines on Sir Willow-Wood's forehead deepened. 'I suppose that's possible. But who would that be?'

There was a long pause.

'Victor,' Lady Violet said. 'What if we carried the spittle here in Victor's butter churn?'

Another murmur chased through the dragons. Even Sir Willow-Wood's eyes flashed with excitement.

'We've got to try it.'

Sir Willow-Wood pointed to two dragons. 'Go to Victor's room and ask for his butter churn. I'm sure he'll give it to you when he knows what it's for. If he's not there, take it anyway. He'll understand. Just make sure the guards don't see you.'

The dragons nodded and prepared to fly.

'I'll talk to the Knowledge Worm.' Sir Gideon's wings glowed orange. 'Bring the churn straight to me at the Anywhere Office.'

'I'm coming with you,' Hattie said.

'You have to stay with the Guild.'

No. Hattie wasn't going to come this far and have Sir Gideon stop her seeing if her idea worked. 'Remember what Victor said. You promised to stay with me,' she said.

Sir Gideon scowled. 'He shouldn't have made me do that in front of you.' Then he softened. 'You can come to the Anywhere Office, but only you and I will go inside. The dragons who take you there will have to stay at the door. The Knowledge Worm doesn't take kindly to crowds.'

Without waiting for her response, he shook out his wings and set off, hardly giving her any time to be pleased at her small victory. And, before she realised what was happening, Hattie's dragons followed, flying steadily until finally they were at the end of the drawbridge, where they set Hattie down.

'Why don't we just take the spittle from the streams without telling the Knowledge Worm?' Hattie asked as she looked down at the moat. She hoped her legs would hurry up and get used to being on land again.

'We can't risk it. We'd have to dip the churn, and we could end up splashing ourselves. That would be very, very nasty. We've got to go inside.' With that, Sir Gideon flew over the drawbridge and knocked on the Anywhere Office's door.

32

Inside the Anywhere Office, the paper towers shifted as the great wooden door swung open. They leaned as Hattie and Sir Gideon entered, shuddering with every footstep Hattie took. They swayed and tottered. They pulsed and flexed. They were like shifting dunes. And yet they never fell.

In the middle of the great space in front of them, deep within the tilting paper labyrinth, the Knowledge Worm's neck extended above one of the paper pillars.

'Sir Gideon,' she said as she saw him. Then her eyes focused on Hattie. 'The human-realm girl.' She spoke as if she was pointing Hattie out as something interesting.

'We've come to ask a favour,' Sir Gideon started.

The Knowledge Worm ignored him and nodded to Hattie. 'Here, human-realm girl. What are you doing back?'

'I've come with Sir Gideon.'

'Let me explain,' Sir Gideon said.

'The human-realm girl will explain.'

'But it's better if I ...'

'Sir Gideon, the last I saw of you two, you were running

illegally from this office. Do as I say, unless you want me to call the guards.'

Sir Gideon bowed his head as Hattie wished she could disappear into one of the paper pillars.

'Into the light, human-realm girl. I want to see you properly.' The pillars nearest to Hattie drew apart, creating a pathway to the Knowledge Worm's vast desk. She turned her lamp so it shone straight into Hattie's face. Hattie shifted awkwardly as the creature took in everything about her. No part of her missed the Knowledge Worm's scrutiny.

'Speak.'

'We've come to ask if we can take some of your spittle.'

The Knowledge Worm wheezed, and a drop of saliva dribbled down her chin. Her tongue swept across her face to recapture it. 'The poisoned spittle, I presume. What for?'

'We need it to rescue Lady Serena.'

'Lady Serena needs rescuing?' The Knowledge Worm shot a look at Sir Gideon to see if this was true. 'If I'd had to predict, I would have said you were the one who would need to be rescued.'

'Lord Mortimer threw her into a cell because Arthur isn't Nimbus.'

The Knowledge Worm frowned. 'This is unexpected,' she said slowly. 'And you're sure you're not lying to me? I can find out.'

'It's all true.'

'The last time I heard, it was you who was in a cell, human-realm child.'

'Arthur came and rescued me.'

'And now you want to do a spot of rescuing yourself.' The Knowledge Worm looked up into the rafters. 'Why don't you storm the cell? That's what dragons normally do.'

'It's lava iron.' Sir Gideon broke his silence.

'Tricky,' the Knowledge Worm said. 'But someone thought to come here for my spittle. That was clever.'

'That was me.'

The Knowledge Worm stared hard at Hattie. 'You're an interesting child.' She paused. 'It's possible,' she said. 'It might be the only thing that could get through lava iron. But it will never do.'

Hattie closed her fists. The Knowledge Worm mustn't find a problem with the plan now.

'You'll never be able to take the spittle away.'

'We've thought of that. We thought we could take it in Victor's butter churn.'

There was a noise outside, and the two dragons who'd been sent to Victor's room flew into the Anywhere Office. Between them they carried the metal churn. They put it down and flew away.

'Will you do it?' Sir Gideon asked.

'Knowledge doesn't take sides. Lord Mortimer doesn't interfere with my work here, and that's how I like it.'

'But sometimes you have to take sides. When it's the right thing to do.' The words tumbled out of Hattie's mouth before she had time to think about them.

The Knowledge Worm's attention switched back to her. 'What do you know about doing the right thing, human child?'

'Not much,' Hattie admitted. 'I worry that I might do the wrong thing quite a lot. But this is the right thing. You've got to see that.'

The Knowledge Worm shifted her neck so the wattle under her chin swung back and forth. She almost smiled. 'You are indeed interesting, human-realm child. Very well, I'll allow it. But I'll always deny to Lord Mortimer that I helped you. And if you tell him, I'll condemn you.'

Despite the fact they were getting what they'd come for, Hattie shivered. She'd been concentrating on Arthur and the children, trying hard not to think about what Lord Mortimer might do to them if he knew her plan.

'Sir Gideon and Hattie Brown, bring the churn to me.' The Knowledge Worm heaved her way to the spittoon. 'Hold it tight.' She sucked up some of the spittle that hadn't yet drained through to the moat below and spat it into the churn. It sizzled as though the bottom was red hot.

'Don't drop it.' Sir Gideon steadied the handle as Hattie flinched.

The Knowledge Worm lowered her lips into the spittoon again. This time, the churn groaned when she spat into it. Next came a terrible cracking noise, as if it was about to split apart.

Hattie clung to the handle. 'Do something,' she said.

'I can't,' Sir Gideon said.

'Think about the person who means most to you in the whole world and say their name out loud,' the Knowledge Worm told them.

The groaning was getting louder. A crack appeared on the lip of the churn. It began to move down.

'Say the name,' the Knowledge Worm shouted.

Hattie closed her eyes. The churn was vibrating in her hand. The cracking sound tore at her ears. She pictured her mother smiling at her. A happy mother — the one she remembered from the good times.

'Say the name.'

'My mother — Stella Brown.'

The shuddering in her hand stopped. Relief flooded over her. She opened her eyes and let herself breathe. But then she saw it. The crack was still growing. It was just a tiny flaw crawling down the side of the churn, but it would be enough to let the spittle out.

'Say your name, Sir Gideon,' she called.

Sir Gideon's eyes were full of horror.

'You've got to say the name of the person who means the most to you, otherwise the churn will break.'

Sir Gideon was shaking. He couldn't look her in the eye.

'Say it.'

He shook his head.

'Say it.'

'Victor.'

Hattie looked at the churn. The crack kept growing.

'You're lying. Say the name. You're going to kill us both.'

Sir Gideon screwed up his face.

'The name, say it now.'

He shuddered.

'Now!'

'Lady Serena,' Sir Gideon screamed.

The cracking sound stopped. The flaw was mending itself in front of her eyes. Soon the churn was complete again.

Sir Gideon looked around him, furious. 'Never tell anyone I said that,' he growled.

33

The dragons holding Hattie flew carefully behind Sir Gideon. Very, very carefully. There were no jolts or bumps. There was no speeding up or slowing down. They flew steadily so the spittle in the bottom of the churn wouldn't slop or swill or splash or spit. It mustn't be disturbed.

Hattie held the churn's handle with both hands and gripped it so firmly her knuckles hurt. She didn't know if she could keep on holding anything this tightly but she didn't dare loosen her hands, even when Lady Violet said, 'There's the Keep. Not long now, Hattie.'

Sir Gideon didn't seem to notice how hard Hattie was trying. She'd only heard him say one thing as they flew. He'd asked the two dragons who'd collected the churn whether they'd seen Victor. When they said no, his expression didn't change. He just ploughed on, leading their flight back.

He only broke his silence when they got close to the tower. 'Go and find out what the Cloud Keeper is doing,' he told the two dragons. 'We don't want him to see what we're up to and have him alert the guards.'

They disappeared and came back a little while later. 'He's asleep and snoring,' they reported.

'That's good,' Sir Gideon said. 'Let's fly to the others. Don't look down, Hattie.'

But, of course, she couldn't be told that and not look down. And she saw what it was that Sir Gideon didn't want her to see. Below, the upturned faces of the Hundredth Children gazed at them through the roof of the compound. Their faces were gaunt. Their clothes were ragged and stained. Their fingers were raw from clawing at the mesh above their heads.

Hattie scanned the haunted faces. Not there. Not there. Not there. And then she saw it — Arthur's face. It was Arthur, she was sure of that. But he didn't look like the Arthur she knew. His expression wasn't as vacant as the others in the compound, but there was something distant about him.

'Oh, Arthur!' But it was more than the shock of seeing Arthur like this that made her call out. That look. That look was the same one on her mother's face when The Gloom had got her. The churn jolted in Hattie's grip as she fought back her tears.

'No!' Lady Violet yelled.

The spittle sloshed to the right.

'No!'

The spittle sloshed to the left.

'No!' Sir Gideon dived to the churn's side. The waves of spittle began to subside.

'I told you not to look down.'

'I'm sorry. I couldn't help it.' Hattie blinked hard so they wouldn't notice the tears in her eyes. 'Did any of it spill?'

'Luckily it didn't, no thanks to you.'

'But Arthur's down there.'

'That's exactly why I told you not to look. We can't get distracted.' Sir Gideon nodded at the dragons supporting Hattie and they moved off.

Hattie closed her eyes and concentrated on holding the churn steady. She thought about her 13 times table. She tried to remember how to spell Mississippi. She counted backwards from 347. She recalled all the countries of Europe in alphabetical order. She filled her head with anything so as not to think of Arthur or the caged children or her mother. And she only allowed herself to stop as the dragons glided round a box. They were studying it so intently, Hattie was sure it must be where Lady Serena was being held. She studied it, too. Although it was metal, it was unlike any metal that Hattie had seen before. It was the colour of a black-red scab.

Sir Gideon landed on its top. 'Lady Serena,' he called out. 'It is I, Sir Gideon. I have returned to help you.'

Hattie wasn't sure if she could hear anything from the box, but Sir Gideon seemed satisfied. 'She's still there,' he announced.

'Lady Serena, we've brought spittle from the Knowledge Worm to help release you.'

This time, Hattie thought she heard a tiny sound.

'Lady Serena, we're going to use the spittle to break the lock on the door. Stand away from the front of the cell so you don't get hurt. Do you understand?'

This time there was definitely a sound.

'She knows what to do.' Sir Gideon indicated to the dragons who were still holding Hattie. They held her over the entrance to the box cell.

'We'll put a drop of spittle on the lava-iron lock.' Sir Gideon flew under the bottom of the churn and very, very slowly lifted it up. Within the churn, the spittle fizzed.

183

Sir Gideon inched the churn up some more. A tiny globule teetered on the lip of the churn. Sir Gideon gave the churn the tiniest nudge. The globule fell from the churn's lip and splashed on to the lock.

Nothing happened.

The blood surged through Hattie's body. It had to work. They didn't have another plan if this one failed.

Still nothing happened.

Her mouth went dry. Lady Serena, Arthur, and the Hundredth Children would be Lord Mortimer's prisoners forever, and there was nothing she could do about it. 'Let's put more on,' she urged.

'That won't help. It's either going to work or not.' Sir Gideon's voice was tight, as though he thought they were bound to fail.

The seconds went by, each one seeming longer than the last. Still nothing happened.

Then there was sizzling as the lock began to melt. Red liquid oozed from it like drops of blood. And, with a crack, the doors sprang apart, and Lady Serena flew out of the cell.

Hattie's breath came back to her.

'Brother and sister dragons,' Lady Serena started as the dragons set Hattie and the churn very gently down on the ground. 'I thank you.'

Sir Gideon flew proudly towards her. A satisfied smile played on his mouth.

'I knew the Guild wouldn't let me down. I knew the Guild would rescue one of their members.'

Sir Gideon puffed out his chest. 'Lady Serena, I have the honour of liberating you from the cell.'

She smiled at him distantly, as she shook out her wings, stretching them as though she was enjoying every centimetre of freedom.

'Shall I tell you how I rescued you?' he asked.

'Later,' she said. 'When I've thanked Sir Willow-Wood.'

Sir Gideon frowned. 'Why would you thank Sir Willow-Wood?'

'For organising my rescue.' She smiled at him indulgently. 'Of course, I'm grateful to you Sir Gideon for bringing the spittle. But I must thank Sir Willow-Wood for mobilising the Guild.'

She shook out her wings one last time before flying away with Lady Violet and the other dragons, leaving only Sir Gideon and Hattie behind.

Sir Gideon's scales went from yellow to orange to vermillion. He turned to Hattie. She couldn't make out if the unfamiliar look in his eyes was sadness or anger.

'Hattie Brown, you and I are going to free the Hundredth Children.'

34

'I'm sorry about Lady Serena,' Hattie said as she and Sir Gideon carried the churn between them to the compound where the Hundredth Children were being kept.

'Don't be. It's nothing.' Sir Gideon held his head away from her so she couldn't see his face.

'And what will Somewhere-Nowhere do without the Hundredth Children?'

'The reservoirs are full. That gives us time. And if Victor thinks it will be fine, it probably will be.'

Yes, it probably would be, Hattie thought, because everyone in Somewhere-Nowhere seemed to have such faith in Victor. But even so, when they'd freed the Hundredth Children, there was one more thing Hattie thought she should do. Only she wasn't going to tell Sir Gideon, just in case he tried to stop her.

They turned a corner and a shiver went down Hattie's spine. In front of them was the compound. Its boundary ran as far as Hattie could see. As they approached, a group of Hundredth Children staggered

186

towards them. Their hands reached out through the bars of their prison.

'Don't let them touch the churn,' Sir Gideon hissed.

With every step Hattie walked, more bodies were being pressed up against the bars. Somehow the news had got around. The Hundredth Children were letting each other know about Hattie and Sir Gideon's arrival. Even though the pollen scattered within the compound had subdued them, it hadn't taken their minds away completely.

The ghostly crowd shadowed them until they reached a gate that was locked with an elaborate, heavy padlock.

'More lava iron,' Sir Gideon said. 'That won't hold us up for long.' He flew to the bottom of the churn as Hattie raised it up. 'You know what to do,' he said.

Hattie tipped the churn very, very slowly towards the lock, while Sir Gideon steadied its base.

'It's a shame Victor isn't here to see this.' But, even as the words were leaving her mouth, Hattie regretted it. Sir Gideon flinched and the churn juddered. A drop of spittle fell near Hattie's right boot. It tore through the ground, leaving a smouldering hole.

'Be careful,' Sir Gideon snapped. 'Be careful what you say and what you do.'

'I'm sorry. I didn't mean to.'

'When will humans from your realm start thinking before they speak? Now, gently this time.'

Hattie took a deep breath and tried to concentrate. She mustn't do anything dangerous. She tipped the churn again. The force of Sir Gideon's steady pressure pushed it higher. A globule of spittle rolled towards the lip of the churn. Hattie aimed it at the padlock. The globule fell like quick-silver on to the metal. It sat glistening on the top of the lock for a few moments, then the whole lock melted.

'Satisfying,' Sir Gideon said. He turned to address the children nearest to the gate. 'Wait for us to return before you come through.' Then together, they carefully took the churn to an area far away from the main gate.

'Now let's free them,' Sir Gideon cried when it was safely on the ground.

This time Hattie ran. She sprinted to the gate and flung it open, until it snapped back on its hinges.

'You're free!' she cried. 'You can go home.'

The Hundredth Children didn't move.

'You're free. We're taking you home.'

The Hundredth Children just stared at her with large vacant eyes.

'Please come.' She heard the desperation in her voice and turned to Sir Gideon. He was shaking his head. 'It's the pollen,' he said. 'We need to get them out of the compound.'

She walked through the open gate with Sir Gideon at her shoulder.

'Come on. Come on. You're free.' They passed through the crowd, pointing and shooing. But instead of moving to the gate, the Hundredth Children just followed, silently pacing after them, their faces impassive and spectral.

'Please go. You don't have to stay here. You're free.' Hattie was sure her voice would crack any moment. Why didn't they move? But the Hundredth Children just silently followed her into the centre of the compound.

'Hattie.' Out of the ghostly silence came a voice she knew.

She swung round. 'Arthur.'

'I'm so glad to see you,' he said. 'This is where they sent me when Lord Mortimer threw me out. I'm frightened if I stay here too long, I'm going to become like them.' He gestured at the children around him. 'I could feel it beginning to happen.'

'I've come to rescue you, just like you rescued me,' Hattie said.

Arthur flung his arms around her as she heard a cough at her shoulder.

'And Sir Gideon's here to rescue you, too.'

'Thank you, Sir Gideon. I knew I wouldn't be abandoned. We'll have to find Lady Serena, too.'

'We've freed her already.'

'Where is she?' Arthur looked round eagerly.

Sir Gideon snorted. 'She's gone back to the Guild.'

'Without waiting for me?' Arthur didn't disguise his surprise. His face hardened. 'Let's get out of here.'

'But they won't go.' Hattie pointed to the Hundredth Children. 'I've been telling them they're free to go home, but they're not moving. They're just following me. It's as if they've been programmed not to go, and they're scared.'

Arthur looked round at the empty faces of the children surrounding them. 'It's the pollen. It makes everything feel hazy.' He pulled himself up as tall as he could. 'Hundredth Children,' his voice boomed. 'I am Nimbus. Follow me.' And then he started to march. He strode towards the gate. And as he went, the Hundredth Children parted to let him through, before silently beginning to follow.

And when Arthur reached the gate, he turned and addressed the whole compound.

'Hundredth Children,' he yelled. 'We are going home.'

Hattie thought she might burst out laughing as Arthur started leading the children out of the compound, as though he was the Pied Piper of Hamelin, not Arthur from Manchester. They might actually do it, she thought. She and Arthur might actually free the Hundredth Children and get them home. She looked about her, grinning hard. Even the red dust under her feet seemed beautiful now she felt this good. She turned to check that all the children were moving but as her gaze swept past the Keep, her happiness disappeared. The Cloud Keeper was standing in the upstairs window, his jaw slack with horror. And coming towards Hattie, its wings flapping frantically, was a cockatoo.

As it flew past her, it spoke. 'Quick Hattie Brown — guards coming.'

35

Lord Mortimer sat alone in the great hall, staring at a manuscript from his library. But his mind wasn't on it. He was thinking about the Lost Seal instead. His plan of sending the Knight Dragons into the human realm was going too slowly. He might need to think of a way to get things moving.

To help him concentrate, he tapped a knife on the top of his teeth. It was something he'd started doing to frighten his brother, but it had become a habit. Over the years, the blade had sharpened his teeth and sometimes he snagged his lip and drew blood. But he didn't mind. He'd always liked its iron tang.

The door to the hall opened and a guard came in looking nervous. 'A cockatoo has asked to see you,' he said.

Lord Mortimer looked over to the door in irritation. He held the knife frozen in the air, its blade facing the guard.

'Come forward.' He hoped his barbed stare skewered the cockatoo's heart as he flew under the rafters.

'What is the meaning of this disturbance?'

'Cloud Keeper sent.' The cockatoo paused to catch his breath. 'Hundredth Children escaping.'

Lord Mortimer's world went black. His cheeks blew. Bile flooded his mouth. 'You,' he shouted at the guard who was hovering at the doorway. 'Go to the city barracks. Send every guard you can.'

'But —' the guard faltered.

'Every guard immediately.'

'Yes.' The guard scurried away.

'And you,' Lord Mortimer yelled at the cockatoo. 'Go back to the Cloud Keeper. Tell him help is coming. And tell him I'll be there to command the assault myself. No one will be spared when I catch who did this. I'll pin open their eyelids. I'll pour the pus of lanced boils down their throats. I'll boil their fingertips. I'll make them squeal.'

He flung the manuscript across the room as the cockatoo flew away.

'I'll make every one of them wish they'd never been born,' he said as he ran across the room. The rage boiled inside him so much that he didn't watch his footing as he grabbed his sword from its spot on the wall. His foot caught on a bench leg, and he tumbled.

'No one ever sees what I do for them,' Bench grumbled as Lord Mortimer's head hit the floor.

36

'They're coming for us,' Hattie ran to where Arthur was beckoning the first of the Hundredth Children through the gate of the compound.

'We may have a little while before they realise what's happening,' he said.

'They know already, a cockatoo told me.'

Arthur's features hardened. 'Hurry,' he yelled at the children crowding to get out of the gate. 'You've got to go faster.'

But the Hundredth Children's pace didn't change. They shuffled out of the gates, taking tiny, pained steps.

'They're not used to moving any more,' Sir Gideon screamed. 'It's like they've forgotten how to run.'

Hattie tugged the arm of one of the girls at the front. She had to go faster. 'Move, just move,' she cried. But it was like dragging someone through sand.

'How long do we have?' she asked Sir Gideon.

'Not long. The cockatoo has to do what it's told. It'll have gone to Lord Mortimer. The guards will be alerted, then they'll come immediately.'

'What if the guards aren't there?'

'Of course they'll be there.'

'What if Victor told them that the Lost Seal is buried at the caves, and they've all gone to look for it? I heard him say it just after he left the Guild.'

Sir Gideon's eyes sparkled as he took in what he was hearing. 'That crafty elephant. And Lord Mortimer won't have time to get the guards who are garrisoned outside the city.' He almost smiled. 'Then, Hattie Brown, we'd better make the most of the time Victor's bought us. I'll take the first of the children to the entrance of the underground stream and get them to the Time Worm. You speed up the rest.' He flew to the front of the Hundredth Children who'd already left the compound. 'Follow me if you want to go home,' he yelled. 'And hurry.'

The rags had unravelled on the feet of one of the girls, and she bent down to bind them again. 'No time!' Sir Gideon screamed. 'Do that when we're underground.'

Hattie gripped the bars of the compound. 'The guards are coming,' she yelled at the Hundredth Children still inside. 'You've got to go faster.'

The boy closest to her sobbed.

'They're trying as hard as they can,' Arthur said.

'It isn't enough.'

'Come on, come on.' Arthur dragged another child through. 'Go to the underground stream. Follow everyone else and don't stop.'

The girl walked away, trailing her feet heavily as she went. 'It's no good,' Arthur called to Hattie. 'They're still going at exactly the same speed.'

'Can I help?' Hattie swung round to see where the voice was coming from. Lady Violet was hovering behind them.

Seeing her, Hattie felt the same calm that came over her when Victor was close by.

'You've come back.'

'It seemed wrong to be flying away from where we're needed. That isn't what Knight Dragons do.'

'But I heard the dragons say we shouldn't free the Hundredth Children because there'd be no rain.'

'Not every dragon thinks alike. And Victor must have thought of that. The reservoirs will see us through for a while.' Lady Violet looked at the children coming through the gate. 'I'll go inside and get them moving. As they get further away from the compound, the pollen will wear off and they'll begin to go faster.'

'I'm going to the Keep,' Hattie said.

'We need you here,' Arthur told her.

'There's something I have to do.' He had to trust her and understand that she wouldn't do it unless it was important. 'Lady Violet will help you get them out,' she said. 'I don't have time to explain.'

And before Arthur could try to stop her, she'd started to run. She ran away from the main gate. She ran down the side of the compound. She ran past the gazes of the Hundredth Children, who were patiently waiting to leave their prison. And as she ran, she shouted at their passive bodies. 'When you get to the gate, don't stop. Get to the underground stream as fast as you can.'

She sprinted the last few yards to the Keep. The door gave easily when she pushed it, and inside she found a dark corridor leading to a stone spiral staircase. Hattie closed the door carefully behind her, trying not to make any sound, and crept along the corridor and up the stairs. It was time to make a difference to all the inhabitants of Somewhere-Nowhere, not just the Hundredth Children.

After the third twist of the spiral, she saw an open door. She tiptoed the last few steps, hating how her slowness ate into the precious seconds. Her heart slammed against her chest as she hunched, peeping round the side of the door frame. The Cloud Keeper stood inside the room. His back was turned away as he looked out of the window to the Hundredth Children escaping from the compound. He was muttering something to himself, but Hattie couldn't tell what he was saying, and she didn't wait to find out.

She slunk past the door and sneaked up the staircase until she came across another door. This one was closed. As she inched it open, a blast of fresh air hit her. She'd come outside, to the foot of the stairs that snaked around the outside of the tower. She, Lord Mortimer, and Arthur had watched the Cloud Keeper puff his way up these stairs to get to the roof. It was exactly where she needed to be. Smiling, she set off, climbing two steps at a time until she reached the roof.

In front of her, a large wheel lay on its side. Four wooden spokes jutted out from its rim. This must be what she'd seen the Cloud Keeper pushing when she'd watched from below.

She tested one of the spokes. It would need every bit of her strength if she was going to get the clouds out. But a bit of hard work wasn't going to stop her now. Hattie planted her feet and braced her shoulders, forcing her weight against the spoke as she pushed. The wheel gave a few centimetres, then stopped.

Hattie braced herself again. She could feel her teeth grinding together. The wheel gave a few more centimetres before stopping.

'We don't have time for this.' She slammed her feet back into position.

The wheel moved another few centimetres. But this time Hattie could see that part of the roof had eased back. It was just a small opening, but it was something.

'Don't stop, Hattie, don't stop,' she told herself.

She curled her fingers even tighter around the spoke. This time the wheel gave more easily. The roof opened half a metre before stopping.

Hattie glanced down. In the distance, she could see that the first of the Hundredth Children were underground. She imagined them with Sir Gideon, listening as he told them where they needed to go. The thought spurred her on as she pushed. The opening was a metre wide now. She pushed some more. Two metres. She pushed again. Three metres, four metres, five. She pushed again. Six metres, seven metres, eight. She pushed again. Nine metres, ten metres, eleven.

She could see the wispy edges of a cloud.

But then there was a sickening crack. The wheel squealed. This couldn't be happening. The Cloud Keeper would hear. But even so, she had to keep on pushing. She forced her weight against the spoke.

Twelve metres, thirteen metres, fourteen.

The cloud started to emerge as she heard the door below her burst open.

37

In the great hall of the palace, Lord Mortimer opened his eyes and blinked hard. The edges of the world looked fuzzy. Its details came in and out of focus, and his head throbbed as though one of the pangolin workers was hammering nails into it. He was about to close his eyes again so he could rest when he remembered. The Hundredth Children were escaping.

Suddenly the world became sharp. He tried to scramble up but his legs buckled beneath him. He flung out his hand to the bench to stop himself falling again. The bench. He glared at it. The bench had done this to him. He didn't know who had brought it into the great hall, but when he found out, he'd have every hair on their body plucked out one by one. He wouldn't forget. He never forgot.

His legs were becoming steadier now. 'Guard!' he called.

No one came.

'Guard!'

Still no one came.

'Guard!' he yelled. It was the kind of yell that ripped

holes in lungs. The kind of yell that usually made ten red-faced guards run into the great hall.

The door swung open, but only one guard entered. He was out of breath.

'What took you so long? Where are the others?' Lord Mortimer demanded.

'They've gone.' The guard trembled.

'Have they rounded up the Hundredth Children? Have they flogged them for trying to escape? Have they sliced off their ears yet?'

The guard licked his lips nervously. 'They may not yet have got to where the Hundredth Children are,' he admitted.

Lord Mortimer's nostrils flared.

'They were at the caves when the news came.' The guard tried to sound as though this was completely normal. 'I've sent a cockatoo to tell them.'

'What, all of them at the caves?'

The guard wrapped his cloak around himself nervously, as though he hoped it would make him disappear. 'All the guards in the city. All except me. I said I'd stay here with you.'

'But the caves are nowhere near the compound.'

The guard pulled his cloak even closer to his body.

'Why did they all go to the caves?' Lord Mortimer demanded.

'They were told there might be something important there.'

'What was so important they left me here with just one guard to protect me?' A dangerous sarcasm was creeping into Lord Mortimer's voice.

The guard coughed. 'The Lost Seal.'

Lord Mortimer's eyes bulged. 'And what made them think it was there?'

'Victor told them.'

'That meddling elephant! He'll regret the day he did that.' Lord Mortimer strode to the spot his sword had fallen, close to the hearth where he now thought he might one day have Victor roasted. As he reached down, he wondered what elephant flesh tasted like. He raised the sword in his right hand.

'Get me my horse!'

38

Immediately after the door of the Keep burst open, Hattie heard boots pounding the steps. 'What's happening?' the Cloud Keeper called.

Hattie tightened her grip on the spoke and pushed harder.

Fifteen metres, sixteen metres, seventeen metres. The cloud burst free as the Cloud Keeper panted his way to the roof.

'No,' he yelled as he watched it bounce and float away. His horror-filled eyes fixed on the gap as another cloud sprang up. Then another. Then another. The tower was puffing out clouds.

'Close the roof!' The Cloud Keeper lunged towards Hattie.

She ran around to the other side of the wheel.

He chased. 'What have you done?'

'I'm freeing them so that everyone can have water, not just Lord Mortimer and his friends. They may only be able to throw stones at them to get them to rain, but it'll be better than what they've got now.'

She circled the wheel, with the Cloud Keeper after her. Still the clouds kept on coming. They belched like smoke from a chimney.

'Catch me.' Hattie laughed as she bounced round the wheel.

'When I do, I'm going to punish you.' The Cloud Keeper was holding his sides as he ran.

'You'd better not waste your breath. You need whatever you can get,' Hattie told him.

The Cloud Keeper flung himself at her just as he started rocking. He blinked hard. 'I feel dizzy,' he wheezed. And as he sank to the ground, Hattie whizzed his cloak around him like a cocoon and trussed him with his own belt.

'Sorry about that,' she said. 'I just couldn't let you stop me. But you'll be all right. They'll find you soon. And they'll know it wasn't your fault.'

She stepped over him to get to the top of the stairs as another three clouds popped through the roof. But she didn't have time to watch what happened to them. She needed to get back to the compound as soon as possible. She went around the corner, and her heart jumped. In the far distance, coming towards them, was a red cloud and just visible in the swirling dust, Hattie could see thirty guards whipping their horses to spur them on. From the size of the cloud billowing behind them, she could tell many more followed. She looked towards the Hundredth Children. Too many of them were still in the compound.

They weren't going to make it! She jumped the last few steps to reach the door of the tower and shot outside, running as fast as she could to reach the compound. Her heart boomed. As she got closer, she heard a voice.

'Not long now.' Lady Violet called to her from inside the bars of the compound.

'The guards — they're nearly here,' Hattie panted.

The tips of Lady Violet's wings pulsed purple and grey. 'Move,' she shouted. 'Faster. Faster.'

Hattie sprinted round the front to the gate. 'The guards are here,' she called to Arthur. She looked back over her shoulder. The guards were lining up, ready to attack, their breastplates glinting in the sunlight.

'We're not going to get them to the stream in time.'

'Don't give up, Hattie. We've got this far.' Arthur gave her a courageous smile.

'Just two more children now.' Lady Violet almost pushed them out of the compound. 'I don't care how much it hurts, just run,' she shouted in their ears.

'They're coming.' Hattie's heart pounded.

The first of the guards had jumped from their horses and were swooping on the entrance to the underground stream. They picked up each child one by one, throwing them back towards the compound. Hundredth Child after Hundredth Child fell.

'There's nothing we can do to help now.' Lady Violet's voice was anxious. 'But they haven't seen us yet. I can get you out the other way.' She pointed in the opposite direction from the underground stream. 'You can't save those children, but you can save yourselves.'

No. She couldn't run away. Not now. 'We've got to stay with them.' Hattie flinched as another of the Hundredth Children was flung back by a guard. They were pushing them into a tight group, moving to surround them. 'They're stopping them getting to the tunnel,' she said.

'But it may not be completely lost. Some of the children are already down there with Sir Gideon.'

'We have to get them all down there.'

'We can't. There must be at least one hundred guards. And the children are so weak. They won't be able to fight.'

Hattie stared. Lady Violet was right. The guards were moving round the children. They'd blocked their way to the tunnel completely and were beginning to force them back towards the compound.

She looked up, fighting away the tears. A bank of cloud had formed in the sky. It was moving towards where the Hundredth Children were being corralled. It was as if the clouds wanted to see what was going on.

Then she stared harder. The clouds had settled over the Hundredth Children. They started to shudder and then great big drops of rain began to fall.

'It's raining.' As she said it, she started to laugh, but it was a grim, sad sound. Of course it was raining. That was why the Hundredth Children and the clouds were in Some-where-Nowhere in the first place.

The guards were laughing, too. Only, unlike Hattie's laughter, theirs was happy. They were enjoying the rain. Around them anemones, speedwell, and bluebells began to spring up, and alongside them thick shoots of the plant Hattie had seen growing when she'd been walking to the Anywhere Office, just after she'd first met Arthur.

'The rain is one good thing that came out of your escape,' a guard told the girl he'd just grabbed as he manoeuvred her sideways to avoid the strange plant. When he was out of its reach, he tipped back his head and stuck out his tongue to catch the drops.

The sight of him made Hattie want to scream. She balled her fists to stop herself running head-long into him and trying to wrestle him to the ground. It would be a stupid thing for her to do. He'd swat her away like a fly. She had to think of something else. She looked up into the sky, desperate for inspiration, and narrowed her eyes. Maybe, just maybe, there was something they could do.

'Run to the Hundredth Children with me,' she said to Arthur.

'But ...'

'Just run.'

'No,' Lady Violet called. 'Don't go towards them. You can both still get away.'

'Run.'

'Are you sure?' Arthur didn't move and Hattie saw her own uncertainty reflected in his eyes.

'No, I'm not sure,' she said. 'I don't know if this will work. But I can't abandon them. And something's telling me this is the right thing to do. Will you do it with me?' As she said it, she knew she was asking more of him than she'd asked of anyone in her life. Why shouldn't he just say no and stay with Lady Violet? That would be the sensible thing to do. *But please, Arthur*, she thought. *Please trust me. Please don't do the sensible thing.*

Arthur nodded. 'You came to save me. I owe you one.'

'You saved me from the cell first. You don't owe me anything.' Hattie would have grinned, if things weren't so serious.

'Then I'll do it anyway. Let's run.'

So they ran. Hattie's heart was hammering, but her legs felt strong. Strong enough to fight the fear of what might happen. She glanced over to Arthur. They were matching each other pace for pace. 'Stay as near to me under the clouds as you can,' she called. And they ran right to where the Hundredth Children and the guards were standing.

'Who do we have here?' one of the guards sneered. 'Do you want to be with your friends or have you come to enjoy the rain?'

'What do we do now?' Arthur asked Hattie.

'Hold my hand.' Hattie flung out her arm.

But Arthur didn't seem to understand what she was saying. His arm didn't move.

'Now, Arthur. Hold my hand now!' Hattie yelled.

Arthur's hand clasped hers just as a guard aimed his staff at her chest and another grabbed her other arm.

Hattie looked up at the clouds and the rain. Her idea had to work. She'd risked everything now.

'Don't let go 'til I say so,' she called to Arthur. And, as she squeezed his hand tighter and tighter, her fingers started to tingle and the clouds went an angry grey. It was as if someone had dimmed the sun.

The Hundredth Children and the guards looked up, puzzled. They stared at the fermenting, seething clouds. Clouds that crackled and strained above them. Clouds that pulsed and writhed.

'What's happening?' asked the guard who was holding Hattie.

'A storm.'

'What's a storm?'

'This.'

The sky roared and flashed as thunder blasted through it.

The guard clasped his hands to his ears, letting go of Hattie. 'Make it stop,' he begged as lightning flashed around them. 'Make it stop.'

'It'll stop when you're all in the compound,' Hattie said.

'We can't do that.'

Hattie squeezed Arthur's hand even tighter, and her fingers felt as though there was electricity surging through them. Another growl of thunder blasted the sky. One of the guards fell to the ground. Then another. One by one, the rest sank to their knees, hugging themselves tightly.

'Go to the compound, and I'll make it stop.'

The nearest guards nodded.

'Leave your staffs here and crawl. That's the safest way in a storm,' Hattie told them.

The guards nodded again and fell on to their stomachs. They set off, dragging themselves through the mud towards the compound like squirming worms. And, as they went, the other guards followed, crawling on their bellies.

For the first time she felt they might be okay. 'You can let go now,' she said to Arthur.

'How did you know to do that?' he asked Hattie as the guards slithered away from them.

'I don't know. It just came to me, as if I'd always known that was the thing to do.' That was the funny thing about this place, she thought as she picked up one of the staffs and followed the last slithering guard. She just kept getting hunches about things, even when she didn't know why. Sometimes it almost felt like she'd been here before. She moved away from the clouds and the thunder quietened.

'Keep going, or I'll make it start again,' she warned. She slammed the door as the last guard crawled into the compound and she jammed the staff through where the lock had been. At last they could go home.

She was just turning to tell the remaining Hundredth Children when something gripped her shoulder.

39

'Hattie Brown,' Lord Mortimer scoffed. 'I should have known you'd be trouble. There was always something about you I didn't trust.'

His gaze scorched Hattie like fire. She squirmed, trying to get away, but his fingers dug deeper into her flesh.

'Did Victor put you up to this? Where is he?' he asked.

'I did it on my own.' Hattie tried to sound defiant. Her eyes scanned the area around them to see what had happened to Lady Violet. If Lord Mortimer knew she was there, she'd be punished.

Out of the corner of her eye, Hattie saw Lady Violet tucked behind a rock. She looked scared. *Stay there*, Hattie thought. *Don't do anything silly.*

'Human-realm children don't do things like this on their own,' Lord Mortimer said, glaring at the guards trapped in the compound. 'Human-realm children don't have the brains. Look at them.' He snorted dismissively as his free hand gestured at the Hundredth Children who were still there. 'They don't even have the wit to run. Even pangolins know to run away when there's danger.'

'That isn't fair,' Arthur said. 'You made them like that.'

'What's this got to do with fairness?' Lord Mortimer said.

Hattie wanted to scream at the Hundredth Children, who stood watching them, as lifeless as shop dummies. If they'd moved out of the compound faster, they'd be safely in the tunnels by now, with a chance of getting to the Time Worm and home.

'Tie the boy up,' Lord Mortimer said to the guard who'd come with him. His own grip tightened on Hattie.

'No!' Hattie cried, as the guard lunged at Arthur. He pulled a length of cord from his satchel and began to bind Arthur's hands behind his back.

'I'm sorry,' Hattie mouthed. 'I'm so very, very sorry.' But as she mouthed it, an idea came to her. It might not work, but they'd nothing to lose.

'Can I give Arthur one last hug?' she asked.

'That's very sentimental of you,' Lord Mortimer said. 'But be my guest.'

Hattie frowned. It didn't seem like Lord Mortimer to make things easy for her. Something didn't feel right.

'Bring him to her,' Lord Mortimer ordered.

The guard pulled Arthur towards Hattie as Lord Mortimer eased his grip on her shoulder. She put her arms around him and hugged his chest, holding him tightly for a few moments. When she pulled away, she let her arm drop behind Arthur's back and gripped his hand.

The moment she touched his fingers, the clouds above them began to seethe. The skies darkened. The air around them crackled. Her fingers tingled, just as they had when she'd grabbed Arthur's hand before. But it was more than that. Somewhere, deep inside of her, she felt complete. What was it that connected her to this boy from

Manchester? What was it that made her feel that together they could make things happen?

She looked up. Above them, the clouds shuddered. Then the first drops hit them. Rain pounded their bodies and battered their upturned faces.

Hattie looked across at Lord Mortimer. *Let him be afraid*, she thought. *Please let him be afraid.*

But Lord Mortimer was smiling. 'So that's how you did it.' He almost purred. 'You two are going to be very useful to me. You can produce more water than all the Hundredth Children put together. Maybe I won't kill you after all.'

Hattie squeezed Arthur even tighter and a jolt of energy seemed to pass between them. She wasn't going to show Lord Mortimer how much he was frightening her.

The clouds writhed, and as the water pounded the ground, primroses, bluebells, and buttercups sprang up around their feet. And then she noticed the strange shoots again. But unlike the flowers, they didn't stop. They kept twisting and turning, forcing their way above the bluebells, snaking between Lord Mortimer and the guard's legs, growing stronger with each turn. The more Hattie watched, the more she realised that the stems were avoiding her legs. And Arthur's, too. They were moving towards Lord Mortimer and the guard.

'What's happening?' Lord Mortimer jumped away from the tendrils.

'No!' He hopped to the right.

'Stop them!' He leapt to the left.

But the shoots were coming up so fast that, in springing away from one patch, he jumped into another. The shoots seized their opportunity. They wrapped themselves around Lord Mortimer and the guard, twisting over their feet, arching around their ankles and spiralling up their calves.

'What's happening?' Lord Mortimer asked. He tried to tug his feet away. 'Stop them,' he shouted again as the tendrils climbed to his hips. His fingers sprang off Hattie, and he began beating the shoots that were wrapping themselves around his waist. 'Stop them.'

But Hattie only squeezed Arthur's hand harder.

'Do something!' Lord Mortimer yelled at the guard. But the shoots had already made it to the guard's chest and were pinning his arms to his sides.

'Stop them!' Lord Mortimer screamed again as the shoots reached the bottom of his neck. 'I won't be able to breathe.'

Hattie couldn't believe what she was seeing. Whatever the plant was, it seemed to be working with her. She eased her grip on Arthur slightly. The tendrils grew more slowly. She clasped him tighter, and they grew faster. She almost whooped, but she knew she had to concentrate. She needed to get the timing exactly right. She watched as the tendrils cupped Lord Mortimer's horrified face. If she didn't do something, they would completely engulf him. It was nearly the moment to stop. She waited, watching as the tendrils started to climb his cheeks and cover his mouth. Now! She let go of Arthur's hand.

The rain stopped immediately, and the skies brightened. The tendrils of the plant stopped growing, just as the highest of them was about to enter Lord Mortimer's left nostril.

'Set me free.' Lord Mortimer's voice was fuzzy under his cage of criss-cross shoots.

'The only person I'm going to set free is Arthur,' Hattie told him and she unbound Arthur's hands.

'How did you do that?' Arthur asked as he shook life back into his fingers.

'I didn't do it. We did,' Hattie told him. Then she turned to the remaining Hundredth Children, who were watching with confused faces.

'Let's go home,' she said.

40

The journey down the tunnel seemed to last forever. The Hundredth Children were regaining their senses, but they were still going so much slower than Hattie wanted. Just when Hattie was beginning to be afraid they would never get to the Time Worm, Lady Violet said, 'Here,' and they climbed out into the sunshine again.

'Are you okay? What happened?' Sir Gideon rushed to them.

'We had a few problems with the guards.' Hattie grinned.

His eyes flicked to the tunnel entrance. 'Are they coming?'

'No, we're fine.'

'Hattie locked them in the compound.' Arthur grinned, too. 'And then she tied Lord Mortimer up with some kind of plant.'

Sir Gideon's mouth twitched.

'Snarlweed,' Lady Violet told him. 'It covered Lord Mortimer and his guard but didn't touch these two. Who'd have thought it?' But she looked at Hattie as though she wasn't really surprised at anything that happened when Hattie was around. 'There are underground patches of snarlweed throughout the realm, waiting for rain,' she explained. 'And once it starts growing, it will use anything it can find to climb, including people and animals. Everyone around here knows to avoid it.'

Sir Gideon's eyes had widened. 'Snarlweed doesn't usually choose between people,' he said. 'What did you do to stop it climbing you?'

Hattie shrugged. 'I just had a lucky break.'

'Are you sure it was luck?' Lady Violet asked. 'It looked like you knew what you were doing.'

'It was luck.'

'The lucky one. Maybe you'll bring us luck as well.' Lady Violet smiled again.

'We should hurry up,' Arthur said. 'We don't know how long it will be before someone frees the guards and they're after us again. What do we do now?'

'We go to the Time Worm.' Sir Gideon pointed along a dusty track that led up to a small hill. 'I've sent the rest of the children ahead.'

'Was that a good idea? They don't know where they're going,' said Arthur.

'I've told them if they follow their noses, they can't go wrong.'

Hattie, Sir Gideon, and Lady Violet laughed, but Arthur looked confused.

'When you get to the brow of the hill, you'll know what I mean,' Sir Gideon told him.

And Arthur did know what he meant, because at the brow of the hill the smell hit them.

It wasn't any ordinary smell.

It was the smell of a sewer that hadn't been cleaned for a thousand years.

It was the smell of one hundred rotten eggs left out in the midday sun.

It was the smell of a monster's armpits.

It was the smell of a million old socks.

It was the smell of an eagle's breath.

It was the smell of a stagnant pond.

It was the smell of a fish's entrails.

It was the smell of rancid cheese.

It was all of these things and more.

'The Time Worm.' Hattie smiled as she pinched her fingers to her nose. And then she saw her. Marcia's purple-grey blotched body was slumped in the middle of a crowd of Hundredth Children, who were clutching flowers to their noses while they tried to comfort her.

'There are more,' she wailed as the last of the Hundredth Children came into sight. 'More poor, wretched children who can hardly put one foot in front of the next. Oh my. Oh my.'

'Hello, Marcia,' Sir Gideon said.

'Oh, Sir Gideon, what's to be done? Look at all these children. What's going to happen to them?' A plump tear wobbled down her cheek.

'We're going to send them back into the human realm, Marcia.'

'How are we going to do that?'

'With your help.'

The Time Worm sniffed. 'That's all very well, but what if their parents reject them? Who'd want a child who looked like that? Their parents might have gone and got another one to replace them.' She sniffed some more.

'I don't think it works like that.'

'I'm pretty sure it does, poor things.' She hiccoughed. 'But just in case it doesn't, I've been doing some drilling. Just one hole. I didn't have time for more.' She sniffed again. 'It's to Manchester.'

'Why Manchester?'

'Someone said that was a good place to go.'

'That's brilliant.' Arthur gazed up at her, speaking through the red flower he was holding to his nose. 'I'm Arthur, and I live in Manchester. Thank you.'

'You're very welcome, Arthur.'

'Thank you, Marcia.' Sir Gideon looked at Lady Violet. Together they rose up, carrying a large stone between them.

'I'm so very sorry,' Lady Violet said. 'It's just that we have to make it look as though we made you do it.' And with that they dropped the stone on the Time Worm's head.

'Oh,' the Time Worm said sadly, as she crumpled to the ground.

Sir Gideon flew to the edge of the flickering light, where a group of the Hundredth Children were standing, staring at it doubtfully. 'Normally we give any returning Hundredth Children a potion so they forget us, but we don't have time,' he told them. 'So we have to trust you. Do you swear not to tell anyone about this realm and what's happened here?'

The children glanced at each other.

'The life of everyone who has helped you depends on it,' Lady Violet said.

'I promise.' Beth turned to the others. 'Promise,' she told them.

Around her there was muttering. 'But ...' the boy closest to Hattie began.

'Lives depend on us.' Beth's voice was low but powerful.

The boy met her gaze. 'I promise,' he said.

'And the rest of you?' Beth crossed her arms, challenging the other children to defy her. She didn't move until voice after voice had promised.

'Good. Now everybody go through. Lean to your right ear, it'll help stop you getting lost.' Sir Gideon pointed to the flickering light. 'It'll be all right,' he said. But no one moved.

'You'll be going home,' Hattie tried to encourage them.

Still no one stepped forward.

'Why don't we go in pairs?' Arthur said. 'That way, there'll be someone with us as we go through.'

Relief flooded the faces of the Hundredth Children nearest the hole. They nodded and put out their hands to each other before stepping into the shimmering wall of light.

'Goodbye,' Hattie and Arthur called.

'Goodbye,' the other Hundredth Children who were nearest said. And the pair disappeared.

'Next,' Sir Gideon called out as he organised the Hundredth Children into pairs. 'Mind yourselves on the way.'

The next pair held hands and stepped into the light.

'You now,' Sir Gideon called. He looked at the crowd. 'Team up with someone to come through,' he shouted. And gradually, two by two, the Hundredth Children climbed through the hole until finally Hattie and Arthur were the only ones left.

Lady Violet flew to Hattie's side. 'Hattie Brown, it's been a privilege to see you here.'

Hattie felt a sadness overwhelm her. Even though she'd known Lady Violet for such a short time, it was like saying goodbye to an old friend. No one she knew at home made her feel as warm and comfortable as Lady Violet and Victor. She tried not to let the wrench she was feeling show as she

217

spoke. 'And I've loved meeting you, Lady Violet. Thank you for coming back to help us.'

'It was an honour to see you help those children.' Lady Violet stared deeply into Hattie's eyes, as if she wanted to remember this moment for a very long time.

'I wish Victor had been here to say goodbye,' Hattie said. She couldn't believe he wasn't there to see her off. It was impossible to think she'd leave without hugging him again.

'He'll have his reasons,' Lady Violet told her. 'He always has.' She looked wistful. 'But I wish he'd seen what you did at the compound. He'd have been so very proud.'

'It was nothing. It's what anyone would have done.'

'No, Hattie, that wasn't what anyone would have done.' Lady Violet bowed her head. 'Until we meet again, Hattie Brown, I am your humble servant.'

'Just thanks will do.' Hattie laughed. She turned to Sir Gideon, and as she moved she saw something coming over the brow of the hill. Something large. Something grey. Something crumpled.

'Victor!' She ran to him, throwing her arms around him and hugging him as though she never wanted to let go. Because, really, that was how she felt. She never wanted to be without Victor at her side again.

'Hello, Hattie.' The rumble of his voice made her feel warm inside.

'You lured the guards away from us,' she said and hugged him tighter.

'Ah, you know about that.' As Victor pulled back from Hattie, she saw that he was smiling. 'But then a cockatoo arrived and told them what was happening at the compound, so the guards from the palace came back as fast as they could,' he said. 'I was afraid they might stop you. But I see they didn't.'

'They tried, but Hattie locked them in the compound after she'd freed us,' Arthur said.

'Hello, Arthur, it's good to see you here.' Victor's ears flapped gently. 'And how exactly did she lock the guards in the compound? Last I saw there were about one hundred of them.'

'There was a storm.'

Victor's gaze went between Arthur and Hattie. His eyes narrowed.

'You told me that Arthur didn't need me to make it rain,' Hattie said. 'But he does. He can only make proper rain when I'm there.'

Victor's expression became deadly serious. 'It's true. I told you that, Hattie,' he said. 'In the beginning that's what I believed, and then when I realised I was wrong, I thought it was safer not to tell you I'd changed my mind. I didn't want you to draw attention to yourself. But it looks like you've done that anyway.' He paused. 'A storm. I don't think Somewhere-Nowhere has ever seen a storm.'

'It was after Hattie let all the clouds out of the Keep,' Arthur said.

'Hattie, did you?' For a second, Victor looked worried.

'I wanted everyone outside the city to have water, too. They can throw stones and get a few drops. That's better than nothing, isn't it?'

Victor's brow flickered. 'But,' he started. Then he stopped. 'You rescued Lady Serena. You rescued Arthur. You rescued the Hundredth Children. You've done well, Hattie Brown.' He touched Hattie's shoulder with his trunk.

'But now she has to go,' Sir Gideon said. 'Before the guards get out of the compound and free Lord Mortimer.

And before Marcia wakes up and starts crying again. And before she causes any more trouble.'

Victor laughed. 'For once, Sir Gideon's right, Hattie.'

'But will you be okay? Lord Mortimer will find out about the caves. Won't he punish you?'

Victor rolled his shoulders. 'Don't worry about me, Hattie. I can look after myself. But it's time for you to go. You can't risk staying any longer.'

Even though Hattie knew he was right, she still felt a tug in her heart telling her that Somewhere-Nowhere was a place she belonged and never wanted to leave. It wasn't a feeling she could put a name to. She wouldn't be able to explain it easily if someone asked what it was, but even when she'd seen the Hundredth Children behind bars, even when Lord Mortimer had thrown her into a prison cell, the feeling hadn't gone away. Despite everything she'd experienced, there was something about Somewhere-Nowhere that seemed right. It felt as though Victor, Sir Gideon, Lady Violet, and the Time Worm had always been her friends and always would be. It felt so natural to have met Arthur there. She fitted like she'd never fitted anywhere before. But of course she couldn't stay. Just because she felt she belonged somewhere didn't mean she did. And if she didn't go back to Worcester, who would protect her mother from The Gloom?

'Goodbye, Victor,' she said, hoping he wouldn't hear how her voice caught in her throat. 'I'm glad you pulled me through the fridge. I'll never forget Somewhere-Nowhere. I'll never forget you.'

She took a step towards the hole, trying not to catch his eye in case she cried, then she stopped. 'There's one thing. We ruined your butter churn. But it was for the sake of Somewhere-Nowhere. Will you forgive us?'

Victor smiled. 'For the sake of Somewhere-Nowhere, I'll forgive you anything. Now goodbye, Hattie Brown.'

'Goodbye, Victor. Goodbye, Lady Violet. Goodbye, Sir Gideon.'

'Goodbye, Hattie,' Victor and Lady Violet replied. But there was one voice missing.

'What about you, Sir Gideon?' Hattie asked. 'Aren't you going to say goodbye? And shouldn't you be doing a dance now you're getting rid of me? It's what you've wanted all along.'

Sir Gideon seemed to be checking the inside of his wing.

'It's us next,' Hattie said louder. 'We're going, Sir Gideon.'

Sir Gideon checked his other wing.

'Sir Gideon.'

'Oh yes, you're going.' He didn't look up.

'Yes — that's what you wanted.'

'That's right.' Sir Gideon fussed with his feet.

'Well, even if you don't have anything to say to me, I'd like you to know that, despite everything, I've enjoyed meeting you.'

Sir Gideon grunted.

'And I think of you as a friend for what you did for the Hundredth Children. There can't be a knight dragon in the whole of the realm who's nobler. I'm honoured to have met you.'

Sir Gideon coughed.

'Did you hear that, Sir Gideon?' she said. 'I do have friends after all. And you're one of them.'

'We'd better go.' Arthur stood by Hattie's side. 'Goodbye, Sir Gideon. Goodbye, Lady Violet. Goodbye, Victor.' He took Hattie's hand, squeezing it tightly so that Hattie felt her fingertips tingle. Together, they stepped into the hole.

And as the force of beyond pinned Hattie's eyeballs to the back of her head, she thought she heard Sir Gideon's voice saying, 'Goodbye, Hattie Brown.'

But then her mind could only concentrate on whether her knees were going to fold the other way. And if her tummy button was about to undo. And she hadn't decided if she was just imagining hearing his voice, when she landed squarely on her bottom somewhere in Manchester.

41

Hattie stared out of the window at the familiar street as Mr Handley-Bennett brought the car to a halt in Worcester. Arthur was sitting beside him in the front of the car, and Hattie was in the back, her head leaning on the window, just as it had been for the last half hour. It had been a quiet journey. Hattie wondered whether Arthur, like her, was frightened of talking in case he gave away anything about what had happened. Her own fear of betraying her Somewhere-Nowhere friends meant she'd hardly uttered a word beyond the instructions she'd given about how to get to her home once they'd arrived in Worcester.

'This is it.' Hattie lifted her head and pointed to a small scruffy house on the other side of the road.

Mr Handley-Bennett's owl-like face turned towards her from the front seat. Once again, she was struck by how little he and Arthur looked like each other.

'Thank you for driving me. I would invite you in, but my mother doesn't feel very comfortable with strangers.' Hattie tried to make it sound as though it was a perfectly normal thing.

Arthur's father looked relieved. *He doesn't really want to meet my mother*, Hattie thought. But that suited her, too, so she only added, 'I feel bad because you've driven me so far.'

'That's fine. I just needed to get you back. It was so odd the way you got to Manchester.'

'Yes, it was silly of everyone to travel to Manchester for a party like that.' Hattie heard herself give a strange trilling laugh. 'I was so very lucky I met Arthur after we found out it had been cancelled. If he hadn't been so kind to me, I don't know what I'd have done.'

Mr Handley-Bennett's owl-like features looked unconvinced, just as they'd done the first time she and Arthur had told him this story. But before he could say any more, Arthur had got out of his seat and opened the car door to let Hattie out. 'I'll see you in,' he said.

'You don't need to,' Hattie told him.

He shook his head. 'It would be too weird to get you all the way home and not say goodbye properly. And I want to thank you again,' he added as they crossed the road. 'Without you, I'd still be with the Hundredth Children in the compound.'

'And without you, I'd still be in the cell with a grumpy bench and Victor.' Hattie's heart ached when she said Victor's name. Knowing he was looking out for her had given her strength all the time she was in Somewhere-Nowhere. In a strange way, she felt weaker now that she was home. She pushed those thoughts away. 'So thank you, Arthur.'

His wide, gap-toothed smile cracked his face. 'It seems like we've got a lot to thank each other for.'

'Yes. Will you keep in touch?' She glanced at the house. 'Sometimes it feels a bit lonely.' She nearly added 'because of The Gloom', but it didn't feel right to tell Arthur about it now they were back home. Perhaps if they were still in Somewhere-Nowhere she might have found the words to talk about it.

'How could I not after everything we've been through?' Arthur pulled a pen and a scrap of paper out of his pocket and started to scribble a number.

As he was writing, there was a movement through the sitting room window, close to where they were standing.

'That's Mum,' Hattie whispered, hearing her voice crack as she remembered that there had been a time not long ago when she'd thought she might never see her again. She pulled herself together quickly. 'Make sure she doesn't see you. I've got enough to explain already,' she said.

Arthur didn't move.

'Come on,' Hattie urged.

But Arthur was staring at Hattie's mother. 'Do I know your mum?' he asked.

'Of course not. She's never been to Manchester in her life as far as I know. Move. Don't let her see you.'

But he didn't move. 'She looks familiar,' he said.

'Come on.' Hattie tugged at his sleeve.

'She's just ...' He shook his head before stepping away from the window. 'She must look like someone off the TV.' He started writing again. 'Get in touch whenever you can.' He handed her the paper.

She scrunched it tightly in her hand, worried about losing it already. 'I will. Really soon. I won't forget. Good-bye, Arthur.' They hesitated for a moment. Arthur stepped towards her and wrapped her in a big hug. 'This is a proper thank you, Hattie. And don't forget, you've always got a friend in me. If you ever need me, call.'

Just like that everything had changed. She didn't only

have friends in Somewhere-Nowhere, she had one in the human realm as well. Arthur wouldn't realise how much what he'd just said meant to her. He probably had loads of friends who he was eager to get back to. But for her, it was one of the most magical things anyone could have said. She nodded as he released her from the hug and went to join his father. Her hand clutching the paper with Arthur's number on it was still raised to say goodbye as she turned to the house. She stared at the front door. Now she had to face up to whatever she found inside. She couldn't put off the moment of dealing with her mother any longer. But perhaps that didn't seem quite as daunting as it once would have done. Hadn't Victor said she was strong, and hadn't Arthur's friendship made her even stronger? Behind her, she heard a door closing. When Hattie had heard the car drive off, she took three deep breaths and rang the doorbell.

'Hattie.' Hattie's heart tripped at the sound of her mother's voice. How she'd missed it. She looked up into her mother's face. It was lined and drawn, but no more than usual — and every crease and furrow looked good to Hattie now.

'Why are you ringing the doorbell?' her mother asked.

'I went out and got a bit lost,' Hattie said.

'Really?' Her mother closed the door behind them. 'And what happened to your hair?'

Hattie glanced in the hallway mirror. The journey from Somewhere-Nowhere hadn't been kind. Frizzy strands of hair dangled from the slumped mound on top of her head. It looked more like a cockatoo's nest than a crest.

'I thought I'd try something different.' Hattie was trying to gauge her mother's mood. The odd thing was, she didn't seem very worried. If anything, she seemed in a much better mood than when Hattie had left. Usually the smallest thing could plunge her further into The Gloom. But the most extraordinary thing that had ever happened to Hattie seemed to have gone unnoticed by her mother.

'When did I last see you?' Hattie asked as casually as she could as they walked into the kitchen together.

Her mother laughed. 'About four hours ago,' she said. 'Just before I went for my nap.'

Hattie tried to understand what this meant. 'Today?'

'Yes, of course today.'

'And it's Sunday?'

'All day, as far as I'm concerned. What's the joke?'

Hattie looked at the kitchen clock. It was just after seven. Only about four hours later than the time she'd been pulled through the fridge. And it had been around four hours since she and Arthur had landed in Manchester.

'But I ...' She stopped. Perhaps it was better not to think about it too much. Perhaps she should just enjoy this feeling of wanting to fling her arms around her mother and hug her so tightly that she might never be able to let go. Perhaps she should just savour the happiness that was flooding through her.

'Do you want a cup of tea?' her mother asked.

'Yes please.' A grin crept across Hattie's face.

Her mother put the kettle on and went to get the milk from the fridge. As she opened the door, she took down the list of lost things. 'No need for this now,' she said. 'I've found them. I must have forgotten that I'd moved them. It turns out nothing strange was happening in this house after all.'

HATTIE BROWN VERSUS THE ELEPHANT CAPTORS

CLAIRE HARCUP

1

The second time Hattie Brown got pulled through the fridge, the weather had just got worse. Much, much worse.

The wind was the problem. The moment Hattie left the house, it came up behind her and gave her a sharp shove. It made the edges of her coat flap like a bird that was desperate to get away. It snatched up leaves and twigs and sweet wrappers and old newspapers and flung them into her face. And it screamed in her ears, dancing round her everywhere she went. She kept thinking that soon everything would be calmer. But when she looked out of the window, nothing had changed. The wind was still angry.

It was morning, and Hattie's mother was up and staring out of the kitchen window at the flocks of things that were flying through the air when they shouldn't be. Paper cups, crisp packets, and plastic bags all sped past the house, as if they'd suddenly remembered they needed to be somewhere else. And Hattie's mother's tongue clicked disapprovingly as each one darted by.

Hattie glanced at the clock. Her mother needed to get a

move on. If she didn't get out of the house soon, she wouldn't make it to her shift at the supermarket on time. And she couldn't afford to be late again. The next time it happened, Mr Jackson might carry out his threat and send her home for good. It was at times like this that Hattie wished it wasn't just the two of them in the house. If she had a father or a brother or a sister, there would be someone else to help when her mother was feeling down.

'Hadn't you better get going, Mum?' Hattie tried not to sound as concerned as she felt, just in case it made her mother even slower.

'I don't know what's got into the weather,' her mother said, without sounding like she was talking to anyone in particular. 'It just hasn't stopped.'

Not since I got back from Somewhere-Nowhere, Hattie thought. That was how she thought about everything now — before and after her visit to Somewhere-Nowhere. And in the short time she'd been back from the strange place that lay beyond the fridge in her kitchen, the wind had been like this. In every TV weather forecast she saw, the presenter looked confused as pictures of uprooted trees and over-turned dustbins flashed up on the screen. No one could make sense of it. The wind shouldn't be like this. And because it shouldn't be like this, no one could say when it was going to stop.

'You need to go to work. You don't want to be late again.' Hattie went to her mother's side, hoping this might get her to leave.

'Have you noticed that there aren't any clouds?' Hattie's mother hadn't moved, but at least she was talking to Hattie directly. 'All this wind and no clouds. It's very odd.'

Hattie stared at the sky beyond the window. Her mother was right. It was completely cloudless.

'They say Worcester and Manchester are having it worst. Worst in the whole country.'

Manchester? Hattie stiffened. That was where Arthur was. Somewhere in Manchester, he would be looking out of a window talking to his mum and dad about the chaos the wind was creating, just like she was. 'Us and Manchester?' she said. 'When did you hear that?'

'It was on this morning's news. They said there were strange things happening in both places.' Hattie's mother's eyebrows twitched. 'Perhaps I shouldn't go out.'

'No. You have to.' Hattie touched her mother's arm. 'Remember what Mr Jackson said would happen if you were late again. You don't want to lose your job.'

Her mother didn't respond.

'Mum.' Hattie felt her throat tighten. She hated it when her mother was in the grip of The Gloom. When she was feeling down like this, nothing seemed to get through to her. And her mood could take days, even weeks, to lift. It was impossible to predict. She didn't think her mother could predict it either. Nothing about how she felt during The Gloom seemed to be in her control. Hattie supposed she should be glad it wasn't one of those days when it was impossible to get her mother out of bed at all. At least today she was up and dressed.

'Do you have your lunch?' Hattie asked. 'It's in the fridge. I made it for you last night.' But she knew the answer already. Of course her mother didn't have it.

'I'll get it, then you can leave for work.' Hattie stressed the last few words as she moved towards the fridge. She opened its door, then took a quick step backwards. Inside, on the second shelf, just above where she always stacked the yoghurts, sat a tiny elephant.

'Vict—' Hattie started before stopping herself. She

needed to act normally. She mustn't let her mother know that something strange was going on.

Thoughts tumbled through Hattie's head as she carefully took the lunchbox and closed the fridge door. Victor was here. That could only mean he'd come to take her back to Somewhere-Nowhere. But why? The last time she'd been there, he'd wanted her to get away because he'd said she wasn't safe. Why would he change his mind? Hattie hoped her mother couldn't tell how hard her heart was thudding as she held out the lunchbox. 'It's pasta salad,' she said, trying to keep her voice steady.

Her mother took the lunchbox but didn't move. 'You should get rid of all those things in your pockets. You've got too much in there. I could help you sort them out now,' she said.

It was her usual moan, but there was no reason to bring it up now. Her mother was trying to find excuses not to leave the house again. 'You need to go. You mustn't be late,' Hattie said kindly, even though she wanted to shout 'Go! Now! You're stopping me from talking to Victor!'

Her mother blinked slowly then started to move. At last, she really was going to go.

'Goodbye,' Hattie called from the front door, as her mother left the house. She watched her lean into the wind, sharply angled, like the long edge of a triangle. *Faster, why don't you go faster?* Hattie thought as she watched every painful step. But slowly her mother was making progress. Another step. Then another. Until she was finally out of view. At last, it was safe to open the fridge door. Now Hattie could find out why Victor had returned.

LOVE AGORA BOOKS?

JOIN OUR BOOK CLUB

If you sign up today, you'll get:

1. A free novel from Agora Books
2. Exclusive insights into our books and authors, and the chance to get copies in advance of publication, and
3. The chance to win exclusive prizes in regular competitions

Interested? It takes less than a minute to sign up. You can get your novel and your first newsletter by signing up at www.agorabooks.co

facebook.com/AgoraBooksLDN

twitter.com/agorabooksldn

instagram.com/agorabooksldn